Book IV of the Austen Gaskell Series

Woes & Worries

A 'Pride & Prejudice' and 'North & South' Variation

NEY MITCH

ISBN: 979-8-88653-374-3

Published by Satin Romance
An Imprint of Melange Books, LLC
White Bear Lake, MN 55110
www.satinromance.com

Published in the United States of America.

Cover Design by Caroline Andrus

Special thanks to my publisher, editor, cover artist, and all the readers who picked up this novel and gave it a chance, thanks so very much! This dedication is for you.

And a particular remembrance to Helyn Roberts-Vickers, A. Madison and Miss Novo, for still sticking with me to the very end.

Hello Readers

Hello Readers! Welcome to Book IV of the Austen Gaskell series.

What can one say when Bessy is gone? If the reader was brokenhearted over her loss, so was I. However, even though this is a variation, there are some things that I knew it was wise not to change. Bessy's departure signified a great shift in the original tale, and to alter her fate would undermine what the tale was trying to establish.

However, I acknowledge that there will be more ups and downs ahead—but that was something that Jane Austen and Elizabeth Gaskell were all too aware of. As Miss Austen often acknowledged, the characters are going to get into a little trouble, and then a little more trouble, but then they shall have their happy fate.

Also, important note: there is a scene of physical intimacy in this entry, between Lizzy and Darcy. I know that can be a little polarizing to some in the audience. It was a decision that came about organically, and I hope the reader will understand.

The next part of the journey now continues.

Readers, Book IV is now ready to unfold, and I hope you enjoy the events ahead.

Chapter 1

Fate Being Overturned

S moke...
    Always puffing out from the mills and filling the sky with the gray color that it exuded. And that, when synthesized with the natural overcast that comes from sometimes dwelling in the North—gave me a feeling of suffocation.

For what was it but another indication of the despair and confusion that Margaret and I felt from within?

Can one begin and end when in such a state?

The reality came pressing on our hearts and heads as much as it overwhelmed Mary Higgins.

We were not dreaming. No! Rather harsh reality had to come and wake us up from the enthusiastic cloud that had encased Margaret Hale and I a moment ago.

Bessy! Why her?

There she looked, graceful and elegant, with her eyes closed, but it didn't matter. Must everything forsake us?

Without knowing what I was about, I walked up to her and touched her face, just to make sure.

Her skin was cold, and she did not breathe. I knew. Of

course, I had known. But why did I need to confirm it? I suppose, I just wished for a miracle. A miracle that would raise her from her beautiful rest, that would overturn the great envelope that was death, but it was not to be.

There she lay, so far away from us, and without any hope of returning to Milton, where her friends would be, always waiting for a light that had long gone out.

At last, we turned back to Mary Higgins, whose eyes were filled with the emotion that comes from being overcome, but her face was also frozen over from the shock of feeling such a loss.

Margaret walked up to Mary slowly.

"Mary," she began, opening her arms to her. "I cannot begin to understand what you are feeling."

"I don't know," Mary began to utter, mad from the emotional confusion that was swelling inside of her, "I just don't know." She struggled in Margaret's arms, but at last, she gave way and let Margaret hold her. Weeping into Margaret's shoulder, Mary began to pour forth her feelings of being both forlorn and giving way to the loss that she now had experienced.

When looking down at Bessy, who never had the chance for the life that she deserved, I wondered if I ever had the right to be happy again. Or if I ever had the right to complain about the small things that tax us all in life. For what were my woes and worries when placed on the great scale of those who now had to walk down the road of the biggest misfortune of all? People view death as a release and not a punishment. Despite that it is perhaps the longest and most inevitable road that we are meant to walk down, I do not agree. I will never agree. Nothing is better than life.

Her eyes were closed.

Never to open again.

Never to look on us.

To see us as we came to visit.

Or to widen when she beheld the books that we had that we could supply her with.

No more would she see any of these sights.

Suddenly, we heard a voice just outside the door.

It was Nicholas!

He was speaking with someone. By the sounds of it, it might have been Plato. They were speaking casually about something—a subject that would be thoroughly upended when Nicholas came walking through the door and the news would have to be given.

I was not prepared for this.

When taking a look at Margaret, her eyes widened with subtle alarm. She was not prepared for this either.

This was going to be terrifying. Absolutely terrifying.

The seconds felt like an eternity, but the moment came where the door opened, and Nicholas entered.

"It's cold out there," Nicholas said, absentmindedly, "like the very devil—"

He cut off his words when he saw us all standing there. Our grief was written across our features, and he halted, not even recalling to close the front door behind him. Between our positions around Bessy's bed, to seeing Mary's head resting on Margaret's shoulder, he froze.

"Ladies," he said slowly, "what are yer—"

As he took a few steps closer, he saw that we were all huddled over Bessy. When seeing her, he stopped in his tracks.

We all looked at him in agony. Within our eyes was the

message: 'She is not sleeping, Nicholas. You know what you have to face. You know the truth.'

When seeing that look in our eye, he shrunk backwards against the wall.

"No," he uttered, despair etched across his features. "No."

"Yes, Nicholas," I said at last, "we are sorry. We are so very sorry."

"Save yer sorrys for someone else, lass!" he hissed, moving past us savagely, sitting down next to Bessy's body and shaking her. "She's jus' sleepin'. That's all there is. Wake up, Bess! Wake up."

"Nicholas," Margaret urged, "Mary's crying. Look at Bessy. She is gone. She is at peace now."

"Peace," he cried, "Peace! Who ever said death is peace? Whoever said tha'?"

We were silenced.

"No," he argued, refusing to see the truth of Bessy's passing. "I will not have it. She jus' needs to be shaken awake." He shook Bessy's corpse again. "Wake, lass! Wake and don' leave us here alone!"

"Nicholas," Margaret urged, "she is gone. She finally has the happiness and freedom that she wanted."

"Papa, let her go," Mary wept.

"Let her go?" Nicholas cried, turning on us with a fury. He took two rash steps forward, and I was thunderstruck because I couldn't tell his intentions. Suddenly, a cry rang behind us and a figure rushed into the doorway.

"Nicholas!" Plato cried, stepping into the house. He must have overheard Nicholas's outburst and had been listening in the whole time. When Nicholas's sorrow transformed into fiery passion and rage, he must have felt that it would overcome his logic and reason, and he might become

4

slightly belligerent. Instinctively, Plato came forward and stood in between us and Nicholas. "Save this madness and don't take your angry words out on them."

"I..."

"Am heartbroken. They are trying to comfort you, man." Plato looked over Nicholas's shoulder and saw Bessy. When his eyes fell on her lifeless figure, his expression slackened and turned to regret. "Oh, Bessy."

"Don't tell me she's dead too," Nicholas cried, weeping. "Don't you do it too."

"I'm sorry," Plato stated simply, and humbly. Treating Nicholas like the spooked animal that he was, the next words were slow and steady. Plato was trying to be delicate, but what can you say to a man who is so broken that he cannot face reality? "I don't want to say it, but I must. Bessy... I'm sorry, Nicholas. No father should have to face this."

"No," Nicholas wept, "I shouldn't. I will not and curse any who tells me so!"

Nicholas lunged forward but Plato pushed his hands backwards, grabbed Nicholas's face and forced him to listen.

"Nicholas, look into my eyes," Plato urged, "Look at me, man!"

Plato's sudden physical contact and holding his face surprised Nicholas. And it was no wonder. In a world where man and woman are not allowed to often embrace each other in such a way—in a world of shut-up hearts and coldness—Nicholas was thunderstruck at Plato's audacity. He had no choice but to look into Plato's eyes and lose his strength at being touched.

"You are heartbroken, and you are a man," Plato noted, "you are not allowed to cry. You are not expected to cry. And so that has led to you lashing out in anger, in wrath and ruin, at these ladies. These ladies who are trying to offer you solace. And you repay them with contempt. I will not have you hurt either of these women, out of your grief. I will not have violent words pressed upon them, while they are here to help you."

"You tell me that my child is gone, Plato," Nicholas blurted out, forlorn. "You tell me something I cannot forgive you for saying."

"But you will, because it is time for you to accept that it is well for a man to break. You can cry, Nicholas. Your daughter is gone, you are in despair, and you have much grief inside of you."

Nicholas was shaking his head at this suggestion. It was almost as if...the idea of being seen weak was too much for his sensibilities.

"Yes, you can," Plato urged him. "Too many years of being told to not weaken, to not give any sign of sadness and emotion has bested you...as it has bested so many of us men. We are told not to break, not to crack wide open, because if we do, we will never be whole again. Well, I tell you now, that is foolish thinking. By doing that, it leads to us taking our anger out on the wrong person. You were to do such to these ladies, and you and they deserve more than your misguided rage. No. You are heartbroken, and you are dying inside. Let it out, man. No one here is going to judge you. No one is going to mock you. You suffered the worst loss a father could suffer. You are breaking. Break. And don't be afraid."

At last, in a burst of release and surrendering to his emotions, Nicholas fell into Plato's arms, weeping into Plato's chest.

"There you are," Plato whispered, empathetic, "Bessy was a great woman. You raised a wonderful daughter. Be proud but be sad. No one has the right to tell you that you have to be anything else. Cry, man. You are *still* a man while you do it."

Having permission to do so made Nicholas weep harder into Plato's shoulder.

While watching both men there, crouched on the floor, with one holding and the other being held, cradled like that of a baby, near Bessy's deathbed, it was a mesmerizing sight.

"Amazing," Margaret whispered, "do they look like children to you?"

"Yes," I agreed. "They are boys. Just mere boys."

After this lasted for a minute, Plato turned and looked up at us.

"He is ready now," he assured us, "he can take your words and feel comfort from it."

How did Plato know? How did he know what was in Nicholas's heart?

Margaret released Mary, who went up to her father and wrapped her arms around his shoulders.

"Papa," she uttered, "oh, Papa!"

Nicholas held her and thus, Plato was released from his clutches. Walking up to us, Plato's eyes were soft.

"Go to him," he whispered, "he's had his cry out. He will be kind."

Knowing we could trust him, we walked up to Nicholas and crouched down near him.

"Nicholas," Margaret assured him, "Bessy was always looking for the kingdom of heaven. She has found it. Be happy knowing she is there. For she deserved it."

"She worked herself like a dog all her life," he uttered, "never knowing happiness. Why will neither of my girls ever know happiness and peace on earth? Why must they die to get it? It's not fair, Margaret and Lizzy. It's not fair, I tell yer."

"I know it's not," I said, looking at Bessy, "we will see her again."

"I want to see her now." He sighed, "I want to see her now. No man should have to bury their child."

We sat with him for a little longer before we realized that he needed to be alone.

Returning to our home, we told those who were there about what happened. By the end of the night, the whole street learned of Bessy's passing.

After eating, and taking some of our dinner to the Higginses, Plato was going to escort his sister back to her house. Before they did, I could not help but ask.

"How did he know?" I asked Raspberry about her brother, "how did your brother know that Nicholas's violent temper was a reaction to being unable to cry? Is it because they are men, and it is a language that they know between them?"

"Possibly, yes," Rasby replied, "when growing up, our mother had a saying. She said that we humans are like branches on a tree of life. Men are the sturdy and stronger branches, and we women are the thinner branches that give way in the wind. If you try and sit on us, we give way and might even break a little. But men can weather it. However, when a storm comes, a true storm of epic proportion, the thinner branches survive the most, because they give way in the wind. But the sturdy branches break because they are not used to giving way. So, when they break, it is the hardest. Nicholas, like many men, is that sturdy branch. And he just walked into the worst storm of all. Plato was raised to know this. Besides, he went through it as well, so maybe it's also experience."

"Who died and left him behind?"

"Our mother," Raspy said, matter-of-factually, and I felt foolish.

"Oh, of course."

"Don't you know how that feels?"

"Yes," I said, "yes, I do. We're all children, in the end, I suppose."

"Some say that we don't fully grow up until we die. I hope that isn't true. Then again, who knows? Poor Nicholas. Bessy deserved better."

"Many of us do. But she did, above all."

She and her brother departed, and I went about my evening. That is the way of humanity, isn't it?

Someone close to you dies.

You make dinner.

You see them after their final hour had come.

You take a bath.

You know that when you wake up again, they will not be there.

You put your hair up so that it will be arranged for the next morning.

You know that they died in their sleep.

You lay in bed and close your eyes.

And then it comes to you! It all comes rushing back. Only then do you realize what you have seen.

The emotions rush to you in quick succession.

And there, in my bed, did I fully cry. *Bessy, why did it have to be you?*

Chapter 2

Two Perspectives on a Woman of No Importance

T he next day, Nicholas had to make arrangements for Bessy's burial. Despite the tragedy, life must always go on and we must take the woes and worries that we feel, keep them within us and journey onward.

After the Granger Hall classes had been done, Darcy had come to visit me while I copied my notes. I had told him everything that had occurred. He apologized for my loss.

"Whatever our differences in society and level," Darcy said, "I do not deny that Bessy always seemed like a worthy sort of woman."

"Thank you," I said, still copying notes, "that means a lot, coming from you."

"What do you mean?"

"You are the Master of Pemberley, and the aristocracy does not believe in speaking with a worker in a cotton factory. I know what your respect means."

His eyes twinkled—I knew that I had made him happy.

"But there is something else," I furthered, "a curiosity, as it were."

"What?"

"I still marvel at Plato's intuition. He knew how to coax Nicholas. I wonder how he knew that. Rasby gave a great description, but still, I can't help but consider it."

"I understand it."

"You do?" I asked, looking away from my notetaking. "Please, tell me. I want to know it all. Is it a language of men?"

"In some ways, yes. But it is not just a matter of being a man but being one of strong stature. Plato and I discussed this once before."

"You did?"

"Yes. It was when you were injured. I was scared, Lizzy. I was ever so scared."

I leaned toward him, took his hand, and kissed it. When doing so, his eyes became like fire—ferocious and intent. I knew his meaning, and it was of passion—not coldness. He needed me in that moment. He needed my strength, my steadiness, and my certainty that I would never forsake him.

"I love you," I assured him.

With a swift motion, he closed the space between us. I felt the heat strengthen, the fire of his affection setting my heart aglow as his lips pressed against mine and we kissed.

The joy and rapture found their way into our actions. I felt as if a wind of true contentment had encircled us, the rest of the world had fallen away, and we were alone. I felt my soul float above humanity, finding its way into the atmosphere, into the skyway and among the stars. All the world, the heavens, and the cosmos had no choice but to be our province, our domain, for bliss was obtained in the most natural, whole, delightful, and astonishing way. We had found our love for each other, no sooner or later than it ought to have been founded—established on the precipice of two people understanding each other.

Of two people understanding passion.

Of two people understanding conflict and overcoming it.

No tragedy would tear us asunder.

We knew who we were. We knew where our hearts were.

At last, we released, and I finally opened my eyes.

"I love you too," he replied.

As I continued writing, Darcy still had not told me everything that was swelling within him, as well as had been bubbling over in my curiosity. Fortunately, I was not left to wait in doubt for very long, because he continued to unveil the truth to his own insecurities and inhibitions.

"You must understand, Elizabeth," Darcy furthered, "we men—especially those of us of a certain stature—are expected to be like oaks. But inside of every one of us is a little boy, so very scared of what the world will do with us. Will it push us in a direction that we do or do not want to go? Will it pressure us into being a worse man than what we are? All the injustice in the world, Lizzy, and you've seen it. We're in a world where the only way that a man can get ahead is by embracing the prejudices of supposed 'better men' than himself. I would know. Was I not educated under such principles, having been left to practice better ideas in pride and conceit? It's a very easy path to walk down—and the child inside of us is scared of that path, but he wants to make the world happy. After all, he wants to be happy himself."

I was dazed and enthralled by this. Sitting there, on the edge of my seat, I was content for the mind of the male perspective to be laid before my feet. For whenever one sex wishes to become better acquainted with the oddities and eccentricities of the other, it is always a captivating experience. But Mr. Darcy wasn't just any man; he was the man that I was in love with and was soon going to marry. I adored the idea of plunging to the depths of his soul, discovering what was within, and seeing the horrors or hauntings that were underneath his character's foundations. And whatever those horrors or hauntings were, I would dare anything, defy all, and call them beautiful.

"But the world does not see that little boy who is crying within," Darcy said. "They see the strong man who must always be viewed as strong, determined and unable to have any emotion touch him. He must be detached, in some way. It can lead to a man hardening himself and turning into something thoroughly ugly, because how much of the child can you take away before he becomes a monster?"

"What does the child inside of you say?" I asked gently. "And do you ever let it come out?"

"It came out when I was with Bingley. After your accident. Plato warned me about my fears, and Bingley was there to see me buckle under the fear of losing you in some way. I cracked, Lizzy. I crumbled. I fell to the floor, weeping like a lump of miserable flesh."

"You were not a lump of anything," I stressed, assuring him, "you needed to be comforted."

"I needed to be a boy again and for someone to hold him and tell him that everything would be well."

"Should I have been jealous that it wasn't me who was there to ease your pain?" I asked, half-sad and half-teasingly.

"You had other cares at the time," he said, his tone equally as bittersweet.

"Yes, I daresay that I did. But sometimes, the comfort of another man comforting you—well, that is a different sort of affection. It is the man saying to another 'someone cares that you are here. Someone cares that you are alive and that you are safe. You are safe to bare your soul to me'."

I leaned back, imagining Bingley, who was a little slighter than Darcy, holding the man I loved in his embrace. Just being there for him. As a friend ought to be, for one should never feel so very alone. Then my mind turned toward the image I saw the day before.

"Elizabeth?" Darcy asked.

"Yes?" I asked, coming out of my musings.

"You look like you were just in deep reflection." He tapped my forehead. "What is going on inside of there?"

"A million thoughts," I answered, enjoying the physical contact, however small, "all colliding on top of each other. And that is after many emotions have also piled on top of one another, like many layers to a mountain. Yesterday, when I saw Plato holding Nicholas Higgins, one strong man collapsing into the other, I wondered if that was how it looked when Bingley held you. You and Bingley. Plato and Nicholas. Both weeping over the fate of a loved one."

"In my case, my love was returned to me," he said, looking at me fondly.

"And I will never leave. I simply feel as if I have been robbed of something."

His eyes turned quizzical.

"Of what?"

"I hate Bessy being gone, but I do not deny, that seeing Nicholas there, weeping onto Plato's shoulder. Well, it was..."

"Beautiful?"

"Yes. It took my breath away. And now, I know that you did something similar with Bingley. And I know that it was beautiful. But I did not get the chance to see it. That is another tragedy of its kind." I looked at him, determined to make him smile. "That being said, I do not want you to go out and invent hardships for yourself."

"No," he said, laughing, "I will not do that."

"No," I added, laughing as well, "Mr. Darcy must not do that. Oh, here I am, laughing after losing Bessy."

"Losing a friend does not have to mean that you can never smile again. I know that you miss her, I know that it was not fair that she did not have the life that she deserved. But your laughter does not indicate that you don't know this either. You just are the sort who can feel sorrow in one moment and still feel joy at the same time."

I smiled gently.

"You understand me," I said. "How can you have not known me my entire life and know me better than some people in Hertfordshire?"

"We each are of a taciturn disposition, aren't we?" he said, repeating my words from the Netherfield Ball, "Unwilling to speak unless we can say something that would amaze the whole room."

I laughed.

"Using my own words against me, are you?"

"Yes, I am. You see? I also have a wickedness about me."

"Laughter and wit, even during times of woes and worries."

"Yes. There is. Always there is."

Out of the corner of my eye, I saw a figure standing in the doorway. I turned and it was Mr. Dennison. He was looking at me with the familiar bitter scowl that he had. He was judging me. And Darcy was having none of that.

"Is something troubling you?" Darcy asked, standing up, with all his strength. After all, there are very few men whose scowl is as awe-inspiring as Mr. Darcy's. Dennison's was certainly *not* one of the better ones.

Dennison did not respond to Darcy's question.

"Come, man," Darcy persisted, "speak truth or be disrespectful in silence."

"It is just..."

"That you are not right. Not now and not ever. Therefore, get along with you. And Dennison, the next time you look on her, you will show kindness. Or I will come back. You do not want me to come back."

Dennison did not say anything but only left the doorway and walked down the hallway, out of sight.

"Remember how I said I wanted you to treat me better than how you treat yourself?" I remarked. "Well done."

He smiled.

"Proud of me?"

"Always."

The next day, Darcy and I went to the Hales, and both Mr. and Mrs. Hale were notified that Bessy had passed. While not being a vicar anymore, Mr. Hale was still willing to say some kind words and lectures at Bessy's funeral, which would take place in two days' time. Despite changing professions, he had overseen so many burials in his past parishes that he could never fully eradicate his duties.

On the day of the funeral, Nicholas Higgins had one thing to sustain him as he had to carry on through the service: many of us came to see Bessy before she was placed in the ground. Not only was he and Mary there, but Margaret, Mr. Hale, us Bennet sisters, the Pitchers, Colonel Fitzwilliam, Denny, Mr. Bingley, and Mr. Darcy were there. While Bessy was not especially close to the last two gentlemen, Darcy and Bingley understood that it would mean the world to us if they were there.

While Nicholas was grieving internally, I could tell that he was flattered that such great men had come to pay their respects, even if we were the means through it.

The funeral was brief, and her coffin was taken to the cemetery and placed in its plot. There, Mr. Hale stood at the foot of it and gave his speech.

"We are gathered here today, in loving memory of a young woman who, despite all hardships that came her way, she never abandoned her faith, her desire to connect and embrace new people into her life—who believed in a better way. One cannot see the full purpose of what our Holy Father intends, nor what is the mission that he has in store for us. But I believe that to lose such a kind soul, a gentle and loving creature in this life, is because our Great Redeemer has a higher purpose for her. She is intended for something greater, something better. Bessy Higgins, you were meant for the greatness that is immortality. One day, we all shall see you again in Heaven. For we all know that it is there that you reside."

We all picked up a lump of dirt and dropped it into the grave.

The funeral came to an end as the gravediggers began to shovel the dirt on top of the coffin. Though we did not see her, we knew that Bessy rested inside of that wood casing, finally finding the peace that she deserved.

"Only in death do we find the rest that we deserved," Nicholas grunted to Margaret Hale and me. "What kind of a world do we live in when that is the way that it has to be?"

We didn't respond because we knew he had a right to be angry.

Next to me, Kitty was not looking at the grave, but at something in the distance.

"Lizzy and Margaret," she whispered to me, "look there! It's Mr. Thornton."

We followed her gaze and, lo and behold, Mr. Thornton was standing further along the cemetery, near the trees. He was watching the service from a short distance. When he saw us watching him, he looked ashamed from being discovered.

"He probably fears coming over," Darcy uttered to us. "Should I invite him?"

"He knows that Bessy died because of the fluff on her lungs from working in the card rooms in the factories," Margaret informed Mr. Darcy, "he knows it might be wrong to come over."

Once more, I was driven by a desire to establish a peace between them, yes. But this time, it was something more. Mr. Thornton was like Mr. Darcy: strong, stubborn, will of iron and like an oak tree. But like Mr. Darcy said, they were all little boys, underneath it all. In that moment, I considered that Thornton might be the same: a little boy who felt that he was not allowed to join the others. Whatever his history, he did have the right to not feel like he would be unwanted due to him being the master of men.

"Go and talk to him," I whispered to Margaret.

"What?"

"Margaret, I think he's scared. Go and talk to him and be kind."

"Why would he be scared?"

"Because it was men like him who caused Bessy's death. He's scared that he will always be regarded as responsible. Margaret, go and talk to him. It will help you both."

"But Elizabeth..."

"What?"

Her face gave way to the emotions that came from intimidation, confusion, and self-doubt.

"I'm scared as well. Scared to face him."

"Human, underneath it all?"

Her fears and anxieties quickly fell away, and her face became indifferent again.

"I fear nothing," she responded. This resulted in her leaving my side and going toward Mr. Thornton.

"What was that?" Mr. Darcy asked me.

"I was testing a theory of mine. If you point out that someone is afraid to do something, it is most likely that they will wish to do everything to prove that they fear nothing. It works wonders when you have a friend who you know wants to do the right thing, but something will get in her way."

Nicholas held his other daughter, Mary, as they began to depart.

Jane walked up to them, to offer her condolences once more. Her kind words, naturally, were like a balm on the open wound that originated from Bessy's departure from this life.

Mr. Bingley supported her words. Kitty and the Colonel also expressed their condolences. However, Plato and Rasby stood in the background, and Nicholas made no motion to go up to them.

"It's not a lack of gratitude," Darcy explained to me. "Whenever you bare your soul to someone, you feel naked in front of them for some time afterwards. It will take time for Nicholas to look at Plato again. Right now, he feels too exposed."

"But you can still look at Bingley."

"That's different. Bingley is my bosom friend."

All that was left to do was wonder now as we watched as Margaret slowly made her way to Mr. Thornton.

Chapter 3

An Attempt

When having been discovered, Mr. Thornton must have looked like a statue from without. After all, when everyone saw that he was there, his face displayed emotion for few seconds before the familiar scowl returned to his features.

Internally, it could not be more the reverse. There was a series of sensations within him. Bessy's death was not something that he felt a terrible agony over, because he had never taken the pains to get to know her. She was a worker of his, and nothing more.

Then Margaret Hale walked into his life and challenged him into seeing his workers in a different light. Originally, he viewed them all as a people who he scorned for being ignorant and foolish creatures. Now he was beginning to see that things were more complicated than that. She sympathized with those he had little sympathy for.

Perhaps he did feel guilty about this, but it would take time to sort out his emotions, wondering where his judgments lay.

But what he knew, sure as day, was that he wanted to see Margaret at this woeful event.

Despite her lack of love for him, he still would not distance himself from her. Every new sight of her only challenged him to rise above the pains of his heart and seek her out more.

He knew, very well, that his presence there might go unseen. Or that it would appear that he was feigning regret for the sake of improving his image in her eyes.

Yet, he knew that she thought differently. Whatever her disdain for him, she knew that he was not the sort to pretend he had a virtue that was vainly arrived at. He didn't do this for the sake of making himself look 'better', but for the sake of just seeing her.

When he was there, he became aware of Margaret's heart, of how she really did come to care for this Bessy Higgins.

And in that moment, he understood. He understood everything.

This revelation came right at the time that Kitty Bennet noted his presence.

Then he was discovered.

When they all looked at him, he remained there, feeling the anxiety of being discovered.

Immediately, he wished to leave.

However, that would look wrong, in some way. And he did not want that.

He rested his eyes on Mr. Darcy, who nodded to him.

This put him somewhat at ease. Next, Colonel Fitzwilliam smiled gently at him as well. This encouraged him, especially since the Higginses had already begun to walk away. Now that he would not be in their company, he thought it correct to accost the group. How painful it was to feel as if one was on the outside and not allowed in.

Then he ventured to look at Margaret Hale again, but she was speaking to Elizabeth.

Mr. and Mrs. Hale were still looking at Bessy's grave as the diggers filled it, so Mr. Hale's kind face was not there to help him.

Dare he look at Margaret Hale again?

Yes! For he could not help himself. He would look where he loved. He would love what he looked upon.

Thus, willing himself to stare at the beauty that was where his heart lay, he turned and breathed in sharply.

Margaret Hale was walking toward him. She was coming to speak to him.

Thornton's heart pounded within his chest.

With every step she took, she enticed him, while also unsettling him. For whatever she had to say would not compare to the words that he uttered in his dreams.

Reality is never as we would like it to be. Therefore, the reality that Margaret Hale would walk up to him, regret rejecting him and offer up all the profusions of love and romance that he desired would never come to be.

But he was rooted to the spot and was willing to face his dreams being dashed against a rocky precipice once more.

In her fitted coat, scarf wrapped around her neck in the most flattering of fashions, and her hat, she looked more desirable than ever.

The last time he had such impure thoughts of her was at his family's dinner. When they had danced together, he had hoped for the night to never end, unless it was with her in his bed. Lying bare under the covers, holding her soft skin in his embrace. Her form was so perfectly made, so much molded for a man to love...

At last, she had reached him.

When she did, it was the strangest sensation in the world.

Neither of them knew what to say to the other.

Thornton tried so desperately to open his mouth and say something, but his chest tightened, and all words escaped him.

When he looked into Margaret's eyes, it seemed as if she was facing and feeling the same ordeal.

Neither of them could account for it.

But they knew it within; they were terrified.

Margaret recalled Elizabeth's last words.

Lizzy was right! Why must Elizabeth always be right?

Margaret was scared of facing this moment, despite that she would never fully own to it.

They both looked at each other heavily, wishing the other would begin the conversation. At last, Thornton gathered his resolve and tried to begin with convention.

"Miss Hale, my condolences for your loss."

"Thank you," Margaret said, grave.

"Though...you despise me being here, it seemed correct to do so."

"Why? I refer to why would I despise you for being here?"

"Well, I thought it was obvious. You blame me for her death."

"I do not," she uttered, "don't you know that I do not?"

"What am I supposed to know?" He questioned, feeling the heat rise in his neck. He had begun this all wrong, and now he was spiraling even further. This was not how he wanted their conversation to go. He had started the discord—again! But now, there was nothing for it. Therefore, all he could do was let the words come out as they would. "Whatever I am, is something that you do not approve of. I will always be a master of men, and that is the last thing for which you wish to consort with."

"I came here to see if you wanted to come closer to pay your respects," Margaret responded, angry, "but if you are going to speak in this manner, then I feel foolish for trying to reach you at all."

She turned away and took only two steps before Mr. Thornton rushed up to her.

"You must understand," Thornton stressed, "that we have disagreed on so many things before, that I never know how to begin with us. Miss Hale, please be kind to me now. I don't know where to begin with us anymore. When I think I am speaking kindly, I am not. When I think I am doing something that will make us both happy, you are not satisfied. Every time that I believe that I know you, I am mistaken. I tire of being mistaken."

Margaret did not respond but only looked up at him. Thornton took this as a sign of encouragement and placed his hands in his pockets.

"You really were coming over to ask me if I wished to join your company?" he asked.

"Yes," she answered. "Bessy was, after all, your employee. If I ever displayed an implication that you delight in sending your workers to their grave, perhaps I was being harsh in my assessment. I know that you do not mean to hurt anyone."

"Thank you. Miss Hale, I really am sorry. I know that you and Miss Higgins were friends."

"Thank you. We were. When I first came to Milton, I

was lonely sometimes. Without Bessy and Elizabeth, I do not know if I would have been able to sustain as I had."

"Yes, you would have. Your father always mentions you as his foundation."

"He does?"

"Yes."

"Mr. Thornton, what I said before, of us not spending our lives making the other one angry, I meant it. I do not want you angry with me. But nor do I want you taking liberties."

"I know. I was rash before."

"Yes, you were. I wish for you to understand something else. I have no desire to marry anyone at present. It is not a position that I wish to place myself in."

"But if you ever do wish to do it, that man shall never be me?"

Margaret grimaced.

"Why must you ask me that? Why must you put us both in that place again of making the other one angry?"

"Forgive me. I was being coarse there."

"Yes. I do not know what the future holds in store for any friendliness that we may possess, but I do not want us to go about in the world and thinking ill of each other. Now, will you come over? I know that my father wants to see you. You are his dear friend. I will always appreciate that."

Thornton's chest rose and fell, with the tension easing. This conversation may not have been all that he dreamed of, but it was not a nightmare either.

"Very well."

Side by side, they walked back to the company, where Mr. Hale was happy to see that his pupil had come to pay his respects to his deceased employee.

This only added support to Mr. Hale's assessment that

Mr. Thornton was, in many ways, a better man than he was given credit for.

Margaret walked up to Elizabeth, who gave her a look.

"Well?" Elizabeth asked.

"We hate each other less. I have decided to do something I had not intended."

"And what is that?"

"Forgive him for kissing me. I realize that, in the grand scheme of it all, I have lost nothing. For no matter what, I am still Margaret Hale."

"Yes, you are. Feel better?"

"Yes, I do. I confess that much."

"Come now, friend. Admit it. You were scared when you walked up to him."

"Like I was facing a plague. Oh well, courage comes to those of us when we face our fears. Not from those of us who were never afraid to begin with."

Chapter 4

Another Day, Another Doom

The next day, I had classes again, and this time it was Mr. Hale's. This class was on the Roman playwrights of Plautus and Terrance, who were two of the ancient Roman playwrights who managed to become immortal through the ages. When his class finished, he was done for the day because he had some private lessons with other students of his.

"Will you come to dine with us this evening?" Mr. Hale asked me.

"I would, but..."

He smiled gently.

"You are seeing Mr. Darcy?"

I felt sheepish.

"I know that I must look so romantically tedious to you," I said, "especially since I cannot help but always be wanting to spend time with him."

"No, no, none of that," he assured me. "You're young and that's how it should be. Mrs. Hale and I were foolish for each other when we first met."

"Was it love at first sight?" I asked.

"Yes, it was. And I'm not ashamed to admit it. In fact," he said, removing his spectacles and cleaning them, "I am proud of it. That was the time of being romantic, you know. Not just youth, but from my generation."

"Ah, yes! The Age of Romanticism." I chuckled.

"The School of Romanticism, more like," he said, laughing.

"Mrs. Hale was the most beautiful thing in the world, wasn't she?"

He looked on me sadly and sat down next to me as I began to copy his notes.

"Yes, she was." He gathered a faraway look in his eye as he was remembering happier times that were long gone but also rested in his bosom. "When I first saw her, it was like being hit by a thunderbolt. Foolish really. For a clergyman to be driven by flights of sensibility, eh?"

"There is nothing foolish about it. No matter what cloak you wore at the time, or wear now, we are all human. The heart exists."

"And we have no choice but to listen to it."

"Yes, we do."

"But she was the most beautiful thing I had ever seen, Elizabeth. It was like walking into a dream. And she met my eye, and I was so dazed at the prospect of it, that I found that I could not look away. It was cheeky of me, but it turned out that she found me brave for it. I took credit for a virtue that I did not possess; after all, it was not bravery. It was mere longing. I asked her to dance, she said yes, I took her hand...and vowed to always take her hand for the rest of my life."

I smiled gently.

"I hope Darcy will love me through all my years, in such a way."

"He will," Mr. Hale assured me, taking my hand. "Of

that, I am certain. Mr. Darcy is a steady man who puts the truth about himself before a person. I know who he is...in the same way that I know Thornton."

I bit my lip and looked down, remembering Margaret's rejection. Poor Mr. Hale. Never would he know that his beloved daughter, the pride of his life, had rejected his pupil and one of the greatest friends that he ever had.

"Mr. Darcy will marry you, Elizabeth, and I could not think of a worthier man. For marriage is beautiful but can also be deceptive. Some marry, presenting themselves as one thing, and then after they have secured you, it turns out that they were a completely different person the entire time. Darcy is not that way. He seems to have always been honest with you from the beginning."

"He has. I marry a man who always tells me the truth."

"Cherish it," he stressed. "I only wish my Margaret would find such a one."

I looked away, hiding my misgivings.

"Elizabeth?" he asked.

"It's nothing. It is just...Margaret and I are alike in that our path is not going to be smooth. You see, she knows that she wants to become acquainted with the common man, woman, and be so much a part of it all. A marriage might not be what she wants."

"I know. I have taken advantage of that for so long."

I looked at him, quizzically.

"What do you mean?"

"My wife was born into a luxurious life, and I gave her a simple one where she has been brought lower."

"Mr. Hale..."

"No, you do not need to humor or flatter me. I know how she feels of coming to Milton. I know what it was like for her living in Helstone. I disappointed her in not giving her the life that she wanted. And then there is Margaret. She was brought up in the same sort of life—of aristocratic London society, and the reverse happened. She understood me. She wanted to be a part of my life, was interested in what I did, and wanted that simple way of being. Knowing that she was like that, I relied on her strength. Her will to endure. She became my light—or at least, that is what I told myself. When you have a daughter who loves you, for a man, it's easy to turn them into a crutch."

"You think that you view her as your own personal tourniquet, don't you?" I asked, unafraid to point out where he was meaning.

"Yes," he replied, heavily. "I think I have done that."

Oh, the trials and agonies of a devoted father who now realizes that he might have done wrong by his child. But what are us children if not to reach an age where our parents can share their worries with us? At some point, the roles do shift, there is a great winding in the road, and both paths can cross in the most unlikely of ways. The parent does want to always provide for us children, to shield us from the horrors of the world, to keep us safe and protected. But at some point, time plays a trick on them, an irreversible trick, and Mr. Hale was feeling the effects of it. I could not remove him from the place he was now in. All I could do was give him the comfort that he required.

"Margaret already knows this," I said. "And she is not angry."

"She isn't?"

"No. She likes that you need her. She likes that you feel this bond. That's what she wanted."

"But what about when I am gone?" he asked me desperately. "Or when my wife dies? I just...wish there was someone to look after her."

"There will be. Margaret has family and friends. Even if Aunt Shaw was not going to be there, which *she will*, do you really think that I would leave her alone in this world? We will take care of her. And so would Mr. Bell, probably."

"Mr. Bell?" His eyes lit up. "Yes, you all would. But he probably would as well. After all, he is her godfather." Mr. Hale pressed my hand, affectionately. "You and Mr. Bell. Yes. Please, Lizzy. Always look after Margaret. I can rest each night knowing that."

I nodded to him.

I suppose, in the world we live in, being selfish and perhaps heavily flawed was easier for one large reason: when you are a good person, when you are raised to think of others as much as yourself, you are the one that must be relied upon. You are the one who must wonder how to support others, because that is who you must be. Although this is a heavy burden, and I wish I could crawl into my own world of selfishness, this was not my path to be. If I could do it all again, I would be as I was now.

Some people don't mince words, despite how jaded it makes them look.

I do not mince thoughts, despite how jaded it makes me be perceived as.

"Well," Mr. Hale said, putting his coat and hat on, "I should be going home."

"Tell Mrs. Hale that I said I shall visit soon."

"She will be glad to hear of it. She misses you and your sisters coming more often. You must all come soon, for it helps her feel..."

"Healthy?"

"Yes. Five young and lovely women can give an ailing one more life and vitality."

"We will come soon. I promise."

As he was about to leave, he turned to me, his eyes sympathetic.

"There is just one thing more."

"Yes?" I asked, going back to copying.

"It is very difficult, but I must inform you. Yet, I think that you are already aware."

"Aware of what?"

"That Mr. Hanley is in love with you."

First my pen froze.

It was because my hand froze.

Mr. Hale knew? When it comes to the hearts of others, one ought not to be vain and make assumptions about whatever feelings they may have. After all, fascination is often not love. Attraction that comes from meeting a novelty is often not love. It is a bit of fancy passing through. But for Mr. Hale to say it—for he was a man who had been observing another man for a long while. His observations must be true.

"Elizabeth," Mr. Hale said, "do I upset you, by talking about this?"

"No, you don't. I just...wasn't certain of his feelings before. You must understand, I thought it was a bit of affection simply brought on because I was exotic to him. I was a new entry in his life, and our work forced us together."

"Perhaps so. But sometimes, even in those circumstances, true affection can grow. Also, from his perspective, you are his thunderbolt. A handsome woman walks into his life, she is strong-willed, determined, you work in the same institution, therefore, he has a woman who can understand him—and she is not living in too high a station that she is unreachable. Then his niece loves you. He sees a woman who can be a mother to her. Falling in love with you was something that fate gave to him, even more than he gave to himself. Losing you will hurt him. Elizabeth... if he ever has the courage to confront you about it, be gentle with him. He is losing someone who could have been the love of his life. When it comes to that situation, the disappointment will be heavy. Find a way to be kind."

Such heavy talk—such weighty words. And all of them rung true. It's not easy to empathize with a person who you have to reject. In fact, it's easier to be cold and callous with them. For, if we give any sign of comfort to them, they can easily take it as encouragement. And other times, we just cannot empathize with someone we have no desire to love. My rejections of Mr. Collins and Mr. Darcy were both done without considering their feelings very much at all. Therefore, who was I to pretend like his advice was not something that I had to learn?

Although, even if so, Mr. Hanley was a different matter altogether. He had defended me, had stood by me when anyone else would have rejected me, and he was my ally. Hurting him was the last thing that I would have wished. It was everything that I didn't want, which was why I had hoped that any designs he had for me would have faded over time. This time was different. This time I cared about the heart that I was about to break.

Turning to Mr. Hale, I assured him that I would do all in my power not to hurt Mr. Hanley's worthy heart. He felt comfort in this and left with a sense of doing his duty as the one-time clergyman that he used to be.

At last, I finished my copying. Next was Mr. Hunnicut's class. Another friend that I would soon have to leave behind.

"Marriage, by its very definition, sparks change," Mr. Hunnicut told me as he looked over my notes. "It divides you from the life you once had and unifies you with another life."

"Have you ever wanted that other life?" I asked him.

"When I was younger, I did once," he said, handing me the notes. He didn't say anything, but that always implied that he was happy with my notetaking. "But now, I am so set in my ways. Then again, I have had my disappointments, and those did knock me down."

"Come now, you are a good man. What is this fear of being unable to love again?"

"Miss Bennet, you touch on a great subject. We all spend our lives craving the love that we cannot possess. And yet, some of us are too scared to keep trying again. We would much rather dream of love, where we can always control the outcome in our imaginations, than dare risk being hurt again."

"You are a worthy man. It's not too late. Fear of rejection is common, but to do something even when you are afraid—now isn't that what makes you Mr. Hunnicut?"

He smiled.

"You are really leaving us soon?"

"Not yet," I assured him. "You have time."

"It's not fair. Marriage...the great divider sometimes."

After I finished copying his notes and locking them away in the records, my day was done.

Next, I had to go and visit the officers, for Lydia ordered me to at least make an appearance. Despite my own instincts, she was correct. The officers often came to see us, but I had been guilty of not returning the compliment.

Taking the omnibus, I traveled to the closest stop, got off and walked the rest of the way to the regiment's head-quarters.

From a window above, Lydia and Kitty's faces emerged. Smiling, they waved at me. This scene amused me, for it reminded me of earlier times. Back in Hertfordshire, when our parents were still alive, and we were the ladies of Long-bourn. One time, when I had gone to visit Charlotte at Lucas Lodge, Kitty and Lydia had already been there, visiting Maria Lucas. They had been upstairs, helping Maria choose a gown. When seeing me come from up the road, they all opened the window and waved at me.

This memory was before Mr. Darcy and Mr. Bingley had even come to Hertfordshire. Before Miss Bingley and Mrs. Hurst. Before Mr. Wickham.

Before that great arrival in our lives that sparked a change in everything.

Smiling, I waved back at them.

"Come on up, you slow cow!" Lydia cried.

Ah, will she ever change? Perhaps not. But time had taught me to accept her verbose and tenacious nature. For wherever she went, she was interesting. And now that she was married and her flirtations and adoration was now focused on one man, her manners lent her as no longer being a determined flirt but being a determined wife. Denny wanted that from her.

When I entered the headquarters, I was shown upstairs, where Kitty and Lydia were not alone.

"Miss Bennet," Denny said, his military attire off and he was wearing nothing more than his breeches, waistcoat, and shirtsleeves while his feet were placed against the fire, warming them. Beside him was Colonel Fitzwilliam, who also was dressed simply, and his feet were propped up in the same style.

When seeing me, both men shifted, attempting to stand up and trying to look more proper.

"No," I assured them, "don't stand on ceremony. I know how it feels to be utterly comfortable. And you boys look like it."

They laughed.

"The most criminal thing you can do is to not remain as you are," I added. "So, at ease, lads."

"Aye, aye, captain!" Denny said as Lydia sat down and began to massage his feet. Denny objected to this, despite that he liked it. "I must not have you sitting in that way. You are in a delicate condition."

"Sitting like this will hurt nothing," Lydia said, "I assure you of that."

Lydia turned to me.

"Denny loves it when I do that, and not even my condition will change that."

Kitty looked at Colonel Fitzwilliam.

"I wish I could do that," Kitty said, taking his hand, "but I am not Mrs. Fitzwilliam yet."

"You will be as soon as I can finish all preparations, I assure you."

"I know. Until then." Kitty knelt down on the floor and rested her hair on Colonel Fitzwilliam's lap. Instinctively, he ran his fingers through her hair.

"That'll do just nicely for now," he said, affectionately.

Watching my two youngest sisters display their affections for the men they loved would always be disorientating, in a good way. I was happy that they had found the love that was owed to them. However, they were my little sisters, and I would always remember when they were five years old and pulling each other's curls when our mother wasn't looking. To see them grown up in such a fashion brought the reality even further into fruition. Those little girls really had grown up into women, before my waking eyes.

Yet once I tore myself away from the reconciliation between my past and my present, I remembered one word that Lydia referenced. That was enough to bring me back into the current conversation.

"Condition?" I asked, raising any eyebrow.

"Yes. Oh, I am such a dunce. Why do I always talk like you know what I'm talking about?"

"Lizzy," Kitty said, "You won't believe it."

"I hardly did when I knew," Lydia said, standing up with Denny's assistance. He was more attentive to her than ever. Such focus on his wife's movements could only indicate one thing. Even before Lydia spoke of it, I knew. Could it really happen?

"Lizzy, you will think it the most marvelous joke," Lydia professed, "But it's the realist thing ever."

"Lydia..."

"I am pregnant. I am going to have a child."

I felt as if I could be knocked down if someone breathed gently on me.

"You are?"

"Yes, Lizzy. I am going to be a mother."

In surprise and excitement, my mouth dropped open.

"I told you that she would be speechless," Kitty uttered.

"Well, for goodness sakes," Lydia protested, "congratulate me already."

"Of course, I congratulate you!" I cried, running to her, and giving her the most heartfelt hug that I ever gave anyone. "My goodness, my little sister is going to be a mother!"

"Yes, I am." Lydia laughed.

"It feels like it was only yesterday that you were throwing your porridge at me because you couldn't stand the taste of it when you were four."

"Oh!" Lydia said, her eyes widening. "Then this must all feel so strange for you."

"It does!" I shrieked. "I am happy for you, but I just need time to realize just how much you've grown. I am proud of you. I ought to say that. I really ought to say that. It is just..." I was now looking on her with new eyes and taking in the glow of her skin and the light in her. Next, I turned to Denny. "Be the best father and husband ever. Promise me!"

"I promise," he replied, not offended at all. "Ah, the sister-in-law who will be an aunt is giving me a speech on parenting skills. Well, rest assured, I am one of five. My parents gave me ample lessons on how to do the deed."

"Oh, I must sound so vulgar now," I said.

"Not at all. You just care. And something tells me that this is your way of being happy for us."

"It is. Oh, it is so very much!"

I took Lydia's hand, then Denny's.

"Well, leave me speechless. If that is not a good sign, then I don't know what is."

"Denny thinks we are going to have a boy," Lydia said, "in response to our parents having only girls."

"Do you, Mr. Denny?" I asked, smirking.

"Well, it is only natural," Denny replied. "Fate has a way of playing the greatest trick on all of us. Your parents wanted a boy so very much, for obvious reasons, and never got one. I do not need a son, and by the will of providence, a boy I shall have."

We all laughed.

"Sorry, my dear," Lydia said, kissing him passionately, "But you shall have a household of little ladies rolling around to worship you. That is the curse of our family, and the hand you have been dealt in life."

"Oh, however should I manage it?" Denny asked, in a faux dramatic voice that indicated him being in jest. "Daughters who will be quick to love me because I am their father and protector? How could I manage?" Denny turned to Colonel Fitzwilliam. "What of you, Colonel? Which would you prefer, girl or boy?"

"For the longest time," Colonel Fitzwilliam said as Kitty made me some coffee, "I had preferences, but then I wondered if I had the right to have any. After all, it is not as if Kitty and I will have any power over it."

"You are not being fun, Richard," Kitty said, "because Denny won't be happy until you have made a choice. Your perfect logic will not satisfy him. Am I right, Denny?"

"Too right, Miss Kitty," Denny replied, "Colonel, you would be happy with whatever sex the child is. We know that. Therefore, we know there is no harm in you having a preference."

Colonel Fitzwilliam rolled his head.

"Oh, very well. If it will please you, Denny. I want two sons, because this way, they will safeguard their mother if anything were to happen to me."

"Even when we're not married yet," Kitty said, fondly, "you are still thinking ahead for me."

"It's my duty—and my desire." Kitty blushed under his words and rested her head against his leg again. "But once I have done my duty, I want the rest to be girls. I know they would be lovely. A father's province, you know. Many a man has walked the earth in hopes of having another version of the woman he married. Daughters are the best to keep an old man company, sometimes, in his twilight years. A son is there to remind the wife of her husband if he dies first. And the daughter reminds the father if the wife is gone. I want both. That is my preference. I don't want one or the other—in a selfish way, I want both."

Kitty moved her head in such a way that her chin was on his knee, and she could look up at him.

"That is my fiancé; logical and romantic all at once. How ever do you manage it, good sir?"

"By making it a point to be unpredictable."

"I shall have to remember that. If I don't, I shall never be able to keep up with you. And I mean to keep up with you."

"Ah, do you?"

"Yes. In every conceivable way."

My sisters—their paths would never fully be smooth, but they would always find a way to manage.

The more I sat there, by the fire, with my family and their beaus, I watched Kitty and Lydia. There, in their eyes, was a feeling of contentment. Of knowing that, in that moment, this was life at its best. In this room, without the cares and concerns of any sort of social standards or respectability, they could feel like queens.

And they were, in a manner of speaking. Their husbands were charming men who doted on them. And they were women who were certain about who they were. There were those in royalty who could not always boast of that.

I just wished that fate had worked out a little better for them. There would always be an impediment somewhere—a want of finances and common comfort.

Yet, when I looked at Lydia, and I saw that Denny was

very good at managing their finances, and they were still very happy, I knew that Kitty's fate would be the same.

However, Denny was not born to wealth in the manner that Colonel Fitzwilliam had been. The Colonel was born to a great situation that he would miss by choosing Kitty. Although, between visiting his home, Matlock, visiting Netherfield Park when we would see the Bingleys, and then visiting Pemberley when they would visit us—and all the townhouses that his relatives had, it would give him the chance to not regret anything.

Inwardly, I kicked myself. Even though the Colonel had been raised to wealth, he would never let it affect his relationship with Kitty. He loved her properly. Besides, Kitty was willing to work while they married. All had the promise of being another happy marriage.

But one thing was quite clear; when I became the mistress of Pemberley, I would make sure to invite Lydia, Denny, Kitty, and the Colonel whenever the gentlemen could be spared from their duties. I always wanted to remind them of how close we would always be.

After all, when your parents die, you feel bonds stronger, where you once felt them loosely, or without consideration that things last. Much is no longer taken for granted that once was.

Or maybe I was feeling my own mortality. After all, I had once come close to leaving this earth. Now I felt everything more strongly. More protectively.

When you almost die, and then recover, everything takes on a stronger hue; the colors' pigmentations become more pronounced. You live fuller. You love stronger. Your purposes become more precise. Because you know that it will not last. Everything is at its loveliest because you are doomed. Bessy knew this. That's why she clung to us. I wanted to think, wherever she was, she was still clinging to us. It felt like it.

And as if the conversation could read my mind, Kitty spoke.

"And what of Nicholas, Lizzy?" Kitty asked, "and his other daughter, Mary? How are they?"

"Nicholas is still heartbroken."

"That's good," Denny uttered. "No man should ever get over something like that quickly. Grieving is healthy to do sometimes. The heart needs to be working."

"Yes, it does," Lydia said heavily. "Poor Bessy. She deserved better. Even I felt the hardness of it."

"She was too young," Colonel Fitzwilliam said. "That is the plain truth of it."

"And she was too good," Kitty confirmed, "that is the rendezvous of it."[1]

I heard a horse arrive outside and I went to the window. My heart swelled with joy when I saw that it was Mr. Darcy.

"Expecting someone?" Colonel Fitzwilliam asked.

"I told your cousin that I was coming here first. Do you know what? I find there is something very alluring about a man who is always on time."

Colonel Fitzwilliam chuckled as I moved out of the room, swiftly, went down the stairs, and exited the headquarters.

"Now that is a happy arrival," I said, running up to him. When he turned to me, there was a somberness in his eyes. In fact, there was something that weighed on him heavily. I stopped in my tracks.

"Darcy...has something happened?"

---

1. That last line was taken from William Shakespeare's play 'Henry V'. It was said by Corporal Nym.

With speed, he dashed up to me and kissed me passionately.

I barely had time to breathe before I felt his lips pressed against mine with an immediacy that only alarmed me for a second. There was savageness to his embrace, that I felt was wonderfully alluring.

He wanted me.

In the same way that I wanted him.

But there was something more, something so very desperate about this kiss.

In fact, I felt like there was a passion to it, and a tragedy. There was exhilaration and woe. There was alleviation of burdens, but there was also worry.

For that moment, I felt as if none other in the world existed besides us, for the globe had quite disappeared. Then it reappeared again. But this time, it appeared in our embrace. The world was in our kiss. It pressed against our persons, forcing the kiss to last forever.

I regretted nothing.

Not the act.

Nor the aftermath.

The deep attraction that lay there.

The longing for physical affection.

The craving for our flesh to become one.

It was all there.

But what was definite beyond words was that Darcy needed that kiss. He needed me in that moment. The last time I felt this was when he was scared. When he was so very frightened by something and he needed to know that he was loved. And that he would not be alone. And as God as my witness, he would never feel alone again!

When he released me at last, it took me awhile to open my eyes. After all, I had been so utterly overwhelmed by the power of his embrace that I felt as if it would take me a while to tend to anything else.

At last, I opened my eyes, and I looked up at him. In his face, there was still alarm.

"What is it?" I asked, my voice hoarse from emotion. "Are you sad over something?"

"Yes. Oh, Lizzy."

"Whatever it is, I am here. Let me share this sorrow."

"It is my cousin, Anne de Bourgh."

"What of her? What's wrong?"

"She is dead. Anne is dead."

Chapter 5

The Separation

nother happy moment that was clouded by another dark cloud that was cast over us.

After comforting Darcy, he felt compelled to kiss me again. I cared not at all for any gossip that I would receive at this point. With all liberty, I let him kiss me again. It was proceeded by us hearing cheering from above. Darcy released me and we looked up to see Kitty, Lydia, Denny, and the Colonel cheering for us, from above.

They cooed down at us, laughing at our public display of intimacy.

When they finished their enthusiastic cheering, they noted how somber we looked.

"Well," Colonel Fitzwilliam said, "what is the matter with the pair of you? You both have the faces of two drowning rats."

Darcy looked up at the Colonel and removed his hat. Both cousins looked at each other in a way that showed their relationship. Where one gave the message through his eyes, the other received it. It was as if they could read each other's mind.

"Darcy, what's wrong, man?"

Mr. Darcy turned to me.

"Take me upstairs. Richard will take this hard."

And Colonel Fitzwilliam did.

When we had told them the news, all enthusiasm had escaped the room and once more, we found ourselves downcast.

Yet, to Denny, Lydia, and Kitty, all they could do was offer their condolences.

But with the Colonel, Anne de Bourgh was his cousin. And the same went for Mr. Darcy.

For my part, while I never felt any especial regard for Anne de Bourgh, I felt sorry for her. Once more, she was too young. Even though she was sickly and cross, she was neither cruel nor vicious. In fact, the more that I had time to reflect and overcome my prejudices, I do not deny that maybe she had a right to be that way. After all, if you are born to a weak constitution, and you are not allowed to often go out into society, you might be such a way.

But the Colonel was silent. And that was an indication that he was overwhelmed by the news. Nothing could rally him, for now he also felt despair for his aunt, who now lost her daughter. Darcy had discovered this sad business through a letter that Lady Catherine de Bourgh sent to him.

We offered up more prayers for the moment, but what could be said for a young woman who we could only be sorry for, but never felt much emotional attachment to?

"Give me the letter," Colonel Fitzwilliam said, "I want to read it."

When he requested this, he didn't look at Mr. Darcy. Rather, he looked at the wall, as if a little frozen.

"Richard..."

"I'm fine. I wish to read it."

"Here, let me," Kitty said, going up to Mr. Darcy, her hand outstretched. "It would be easier for him."

Marveling at how Kitty understood the Colonel so quickly, Darcy slowly handed her the letter.

Kitty took it, walked up to the Colonel, placed her arm around his neck and began to read.

Dear Fitzwilliam,

I write this with a heavy heart that makes me even wonder how I can bare to write?

A week ago, my daughter was taken with a severe cold. Doctor Williams assured me that, with the proper draughts, she would recover in time. This appeared to be the logical solution because she had recovered before. Yet, this was not to be!

The foolish man! His negligence was murder. He killed my child! The evil doctor killed my child!

The cold overcame her, and yesterday, my perfect child left the earth.

I made preparations for her funeral, but I need you to be here. I need stability at this time, for I feel—my daughter is gone! Rosings Park is without an heir.

But I must carry on. I must! Or I am not Lady Catherine de Bourgh.

Darcy, I order you to come to Rosings immediately. I would prefer it if Richard came as well, but I am aware that he cannot be spared from his duties. Oh, that he was as wealthy as his brother is planned to be. He could give up that soldierly nonsense and be the proper gentleman that he ought to be!

I shall expect you in two days' time. Anne deserves her fiancé to have seen her where she rests.

Come in two days. And do not be late.

Yours etc.

LCdB

When Kitty finished reading, Lydia turned to me.

"Fiancé?" Lydia asked.

"It's a long story," I said. "I shall tell you about it later, at not such a dark time."

"Poor Aunt Catherine," Colonel Fitzwilliam uttered. He saw Denny eyeing him quizzically and knew it was better to explain. "She did not like me joining the army. She wanted me to be wealthy. She did so out of love. Whatever her flaws, Aunt Catherine deserves better than this."

"Yes, she does," Darcy said. "Bessy in the North and my cousin Anne in the South. From the very lowest to the very wealthy, this is a season where parents are having to bury their child."

"It must feel worse than dying," Kitty uttered. Instinctively, she looked at Lydia's stomach. Lydia took her meaning and held herself. Denny took her in his arms.

"Never fear, dearest," Denny said, "our child will be well. Yes, he or she will."

Nothing in life is certain. But none of us were daring to correct them.

The time grew late when Darcy escorted me home. We said little on the way back to Frances Street. When we arrived there, I finally looked back at him.

"You leave tomorrow, don't you?" I asked.

"I must. And the only way to do it is to travel by train. Then we will travel the rest of the way to Kent by horseback."

"The whole way?"

"You worry about me."

"Of course, I worry. Can you convince Bingley to go with you? For if something happens to one of you, then the other can do something, and can be an aid. I'm sure that if you ask, he will accept. And Jane will forgive me for my request."

"Yes, she will. I would like his company."

"Then don't be afraid to be selfish now. Ask him. It's the only way that I will let you go. I refuse to let you go alone. This is my request. Do you accept it, or will I have to argue with you about the matter?"

"You don't have to argue. You are right."

I pinched his chin.

"I shall be parted from you then," I managed to utter.

"Yes. I will return as soon as possible."

"I know. But please, Darcy. Be careful. In life, nothing is certain, except for death. You die on me, and I will kill you myself."

My order was harmless, and it made Darcy chuckle sadly.

"I speak in jest, but I mean it," I stressed. "I don't know when it happened that so much of my life was dependent on your safety and happiness. But along the way of my seeking independence, I stumbled on something shocking. I stumbled on the fact that you are the most important thing to me. And I cannot be without you."

"Oh, Elizabeth," he said, taking my face in his hands. "You must always mean this."

"I can and I do. Always."

Once more, we kissed each other passionately.

Eventually, we arrived at my home, but I was not ready to go inside. There shall always be something very hard about parting with the man you love, especially when the romance is in full bloom, and both parties actually like the other.

"I..." I began, trying to form my words properly.

"Yes?" he questioned.

"She was the woman that you intended to marry."

Seeing where my mind was headed, Darcy took my hand, to calm my nerves. Despite Anne's tragic departure from this earth, why was I suddenly so very afraid of her shadow?

"That my aunt *wanted* me to marry. But Elizabeth, I was never intending it. You saw us together. Anne and I did not love each other. There were times when I cursed my aunt. Since she had intended us to marry all our lives, it never left any time for Anne and me to become close. For, if you are a child, and you are told, even back then, that you are to marry a certain woman, it is repulsive to you. You can never form anything passionate because it was assigned to you."

This revelation had never occurred to me. However, since I had never been intended for any man my entire life, I was not accustomed to the intricacies of such entanglements.

"You and Anne were told you were intended to marry even when you were children?" I asked, horrified.

"Yes, we were."

I leaned back in the carriage and looked ahead.

"That must have been awful."

"It was."

"But now, it explains so much about your character, and the man that I met when he first came to Hertfordshire."

"What do you refer to?"

"Well, Darcy, you were told, as a child, what your future was. And it was with a cousin, which led to you being estranged from her. That would lead to so much of your character being shaped by duty, old and stuffy aristocratic ideals, and a taciturn disposition. You were never fully allowed to be a child. You were a little boy who was told that he was going to be a husband. Thus, you never had time to learn life experiences in the way that most of us do. You were given wealth, influence, beauty, and power... but you were never given time. Time to be a child who would be friends with his cousin, Anne. You both were let down."

"Yes, we were. I had never thought of this before."

"When you return, we can talk all about it. Remember, I'm never looking away from you again."

"I know you are not. Love me always."

"Return to me. And I will."

"I know. I shall. We shall be man and wife. And when I have you, Elizabeth." He pressed his lips against mine as he talked, "I will possess every inch of you. You will be mine, and the only woman I take to my bed. Never will you spend one day unhappy again. I shall encompass you into myself, and we will never be parted."

During this, he had caressed my chin, then lowered his hand down my chest and ran his hands along it with intense fervor. Never had I felt so complete in my entire life.

At last, we had to separate.

When I entered my house, it was to see Jane there, happy that one of her sisters was come home.

"Kitty is spending the night with Lydia," I said, removing my hat and coat.

"Oh, well," Jane said, "at least one of you came home. I cannot bear an empty house anymore."

"Nor can Lady Catherine de Bourgh," I uttered. This was enough to startle Jane.

"Why do you mention Lady Catherine? Oh dear! Lizzy, she has not written to Mr. Darcy, refusing to give her consent, has she?"

"Even if she did that, I believe that neither he nor I would care very much at all. In fact, I believe we would ignore her ill-wishes, if it ever came to that."

I sat down, forlorn.

"Jane, this is not a good time for parents, in any part of England."

"Why not?" Jane asked.

I told her everything. When I finished, she sat down, horrified.

"Anne de Bourgh?" Mr. Thornton repeated. "Dead?"

"Yes," Darcy said. They were in his room and Darcy was packing his own items, rather than having his valet do it. He had just sent a letter to Bingley at the hotel, in hopes of them setting out in the early part of the morning.

"My condolences," Thornton said.

"Thank you. Of course, I know that you never met my cousin, but still, I thank you, Thornton."

"From the little I recall you telling me," Thornton

continued, "wasn't she the cousin that you were intended to marry?"

"Yes, she was. Of course, I am not happy that my release from her came in such a way."

"I know that you are not. I was just making sure that I was thinking of the right cousin. Other than her being your intended bride that never came about, were you close in any way?"

"Not very much. Our fates made it impossible to be so. I am sorry for her, Thornton, but it was not fair that I cannot feel more. I would have if our families had let us alone, but they didn't. So now, I am grieving for a cousin that I should grieve more for."

"Are you saying that your grieving is more of a formality than it is through sentiment?"

Darcy shook his head.

"Promise me that you will not tell another soul about this."

"Cross my heart."

"Yes," Darcy confessed. "I grieve for the loss, because she is family, and I must. But that's the end of it. And I hate myself for that."

Thornton patted Darcy on the shoulder.

"It's not your fault. By the sound of it, you and she were never given a chance to feel a familial love."

"Precisely. It's horrible when you can't properly feel for your cousin."

Darcy turned to Thornton, realizing that he had not thought to consider what he was going through.

"And what about you? How are you feeling?"

"Let's not talk about me. Your cousin is dead."

"I talk about you because I must. I can't take things for granted anymore. I've done that enough."

Secretly, Mr. Thornton swelled at the idea of Darcy appreciating their friendship.

"Darcy," Thornton said, "I still love her."

"As you would. It is natural." Darcy turned to Thornton. "Forgive her for her feelings. Margaret Hale might not love you now, and for all I know, she might never. But give her time. Then ask her again. Remember that."

"But in the meantime, what do I do?"

"Let her keep approaching you. Give her the power. Women need that feeling as much as we do. Let her develop her relationship with you on her terms. Then shape your development around hers. That's the best I can give you for now."

"How long will you be gone?" Thornton asked, concerned.

Darcy heard the true intent in his voice.

"Thornton, I will hopefully return in less than a fortnight. Depend on that."

"Well, at least I have Mr. Hale for company."

"Yes, you do. Look after the Bennet sisters when I am gone. Promise me that."

"I will. I promise, they will be safe."

"Thank you."

Both men parted ways the next morning. Thornton was off to manage his affairs after the wake of the strike. For he had to reconcile the Irish to their new surroundings and there were workers who were clamoring to return to their previous post.

And Darcy and Bingley made their way to Kent.

In that moment, it felt as if both the North and the South were on fire.

Chapter 6

Grieving Mother

D arcy and Bingley took cabs to the railroad station, took the train to London, then hired a coach to take them to Kent. If Darcy didn't travel by horseback, he could assure Lizzy that he was safe the whole way.

On the way there, they didn't speak very much, and Bingley understood why. In times like this, he could only say that he was sorry for Darcy's loss, and Darcy could only say 'thank you' but so many times. Bingley understood that he was there for moral support and to be Darcy's companion through it all. The whole ride on the train passed with Darcy looking out of the window and watching the scenery go by listlessly, and Bingley reading a book, and watching his friend every now and again.

At last, when they were in the coach, headed to Rosings Park, the scenes were familiar.

"We are back in the South," Bingley noted.

"Yes, we are," Darcy said, his voice lacking in passion.

"I would have thought you would be happy. To be so close to what is familiar."

Darcy looked at Bingley and looked away.

"Does talking hurt you right now?" Bingley asked.

"No. Quite the contrary."

"How do you mean?"

"Well, you cast a thought on me that I do not like. Much of my life is in the South. But Pemberley, and the North, is still the ultimate home. I come to comfort my Aunt Catherine. I would think that I would long to see Rosings, for it is everything that is familiar. However, I do not think I do now. I worry about this, Bingley. For, despite it all, I long for the characters and situations that I have met in the Northern industrial towns. I hate being away from Elizabeth. I like visiting her at Granger Hall. I like meeting with the Hales. Thornton is a friend who has always understood me. Even with all the horror that we have witnessed my mind turns to Milton. To where Lizzy is."

Bingley chuckled.

"What is that reaction about?" Darcy asked him.

"I'm just thinking, all that time I spent trying to be a gentleman, having to forsake my connections to my father's trade in the North, and now here you are, missing all that there is to it. That is an irony that I never would have foreseen."

"And hopefully it is an irony that will not remain," Darcy wished, "it might very well be a temporary mental state. Once I marry Elizabeth, you marry Jane, and Richard marries Kitty, we can return down here often. We shall have them with us, and there would be no reason for me to regret leaving Darkshire."

"Either way, something is escaping your notice," Bingley responded.

"And what may that be, pray tell?" Darcy asked.

"You've now begun to understand. It's not places that matter... but people."

Darcy's eyes relaxed.

"Yes, I suppose that it does."

"Our women will be happy. They have lost so much, and they are looking for love as well. They are looking for something that they cannot lose. We can give them that to the best of our ability."

"Yes, we can. I daresay that it counts for something. Maybe, just maybe, it counts for everything in their eyes. We must fight to make them never feel forsaken or abandoned again."

"That is a maxim I gladly live by. With Jane, I always wanted to live by it. Now, I shall commit to it."

"And so shall I."

Eventually, the coach arrived at Rosings Park. When they entered the grounds, Darcy saw the familiar tree, bush, and garden that he knew so well. Yet, when they came upon the house, with it looming in front of him, he felt the heaviness of it all. He felt Anne's departure already. There seemed to be something grave about the way that the house looked. It was as if he sensed the emotions that his aunt radiated from within.

When the carriage pulled up to the front of the house, Bingley and Darcy looked out the window, at the imposing steps that lay before them.

"Life is not fair, quite often," Darcy uttered, "but we all must adapt to that fact, mustn't we?"

"Yes, we must," Bingley responded. "Oh well, let's try making it out of the carriage, for starters."

"Then what happens next? We put one foot in front of

the other? Yes," Darcy said, answering his own question. "Yes, we do just that."

Both men exited the carriage, the steward greeted them and soon Darcy and Bingley found themselves being led by a servant, named Victor, to the sitting room. When they entered, Darcy halted, and Bingley did the same.

For there, sitting alone, was Lady Catherine de Bourgh, dressed in black.

The very sight of her, after all that time, was enough to remind Darcy of his affection for his aunt. Whatever her faults, she did love him very much, and did care for his welfare. In that moment, he understood why she wanted him to marry Anne, no matter how ill-judged it was. But seeing her there, looking down at her lap, was too much to bear. His aunt was a proud woman, of robust health, and strong countenance. She had a will of iron and a proud nature. And to see her there, wilting from sorrow, was enough to compel the most indifferent soul to pity her. Her sensibilities were neither false nor exaggerated. She was not the sort of character for extremely false scenes when it came to emotion. No. She was a true grieving mother.

Bingley also felt the same sort of gravity to the situation, and his posture slackened, a little intimidated.

Darcy gathered his strength and walked up to his aunt, accepting that his stiff demeanor would not work now. Instead, he knew that it was better to neither stand on ceremony nor to give her cold prudence.

When he walked up to her, his voice was gentle.

"Aunt Catherine?" he asked.

She looked up at him.

"Darcy," she uttered, her voice cracking under the strain. "You come so late."

"I know." He bent down, kneeling at her feet, and he

took her hands in his, to offer his care and consideration. "Aunt Catherine, I am so sorry."

"It's not your fault," she said, barely looking at him. Rather, it was as if she was looking past him, seeing an invisible image that rested just above his head. Darcy was aware of how her eyes had glossed over, and that part of her was there with him, and another part of her spirit was looking at a different plane, at a different plateau.

"I know. But I still feel compelled to say it. Let me be sorry for you, Aunt. She is your only daughter."

"Was."

"What?"

At last Lady Catherine looked at him, in full.

"*Was*, Darcy. She *was* my daughter. She's gone now." Suddenly, as if the past tense had driven her to the edge of any self-control, Lady Catherine's eyes filled with sadness, and she began to weep uncontrollably. "My baby is gone!" Darcy raised himself up and held her as she wept into his shoulder. "She is gone, Darcy! What have I done? What have I done to anger God?"

"You did nothing," Darcy answered desperately, "you did nothing to anger him. This is just the way of life. Sickness takes us all by the end. Except those of us who are blessed enough to leave in our sleep. You did right by her. She died knowing that you loved her."

"But it is not fair. Why is life never fair!"

Darcy gave Bingley the 'leave us alone' look, Bingley perceived, and he went to the billiards room.

"Go on," Darcy assured Lady Catherine, patting her hair, "weep on, Aunt. Weep all you like."

Comforted in his embrace, Lady Catherine continued to leave her fortitude by the wayside and deliver herself unto the throes of despair.

And Darcy remained, to be her rock at such a time.

When Lady Catherine calmed down, she requested to retire to her room to rest. This gave Darcy time to speak to Bingley, to acquire him of the news.

"I am sorry," Darcy said, "I should have never asked you to join me."

"Why not?" Bingley asked. "You do not want me here?"

"It is not that. I like you being here. It helps me not be alone."

While Bingley still held a billiard stick in his hand, Darcy walked to the window and looked out of it.

"I just realize now that my aunt might not want to see anything else other than family. I was thinking of myself, and not about her. It was selfish."

"It was not selfish. You had no way of knowing what to expect. You are used to looking at your aunt and seeing a strong character. And she is. As a result, you would never have seen this coming." Bingley put the stick down and leaned against the table. "It hurts you, doesn't it? Seeing your aunt like that?"

"Seeing a woman of immense pride and confidence now turn into a shadow of her formal self? Yes, Bingley, I suppose that I do. I tell myself that this is natural. Her daughter died; she has every reason to be this way. Anything less would be unfeeling and unnatural. And yet, I cannot understand why I cannot reconcile this with her situation. But to see her so heartbroken...it scared me for a moment."

At last, Darcy turned back to Bingley.

"Anne was her only child. What can she do now?"

Bingley shook his head.

"I don't know," was the only answer that Bingley could offer. "Why didn't she and her husband have more children?

I don't deny that I have often wondered about that. Did your uncle die soon into their marriage?"

"No, they were together for ten years before he died of a fever. I never thought to ask her about that."

"Of course not."

"Yes. It is never our place to ask questions that are worth getting an answer out of. It is impertinent...whatever that means in circumstances such as these."

Darcy folded his arms over his chest.

"My Aunt Catherine finds herself to be alone. For the first time in so long. She is alone. Whatever her flaws, my aunt loves people. Even when it does not seem that she does. She dominates others because she is obsessed with humanity. That much is certain. Mix an inherited pride with cares of others, and you have a recipe for a dominant nature. A caring one, but a dominant one."

"I always wondered if you and she were similar in nature."

Darcy gave Bingley a sharp look, but Bingley was having none of it. Of course, in the wake of death, one sometimes becomes braver, because they are aware that they do not have all the time in the world. Due to such, Bingley knew that what ought to be said could not be held off. He must steam forward, softly, *softly*.

"Come now, Darcy, you know what I mean. Like her, you have many in your charge, care, and you must make decisions for all. It leads to a dominant nature. I have relied upon that very nature of yours. Do not pretend that it does not exist."

Darcy was unable to argue the statement.

"Very well. There is much truth to that."

"I never wondered if that role was hard on you. But now I see that it might be."

Darcy considered this as he remained there, letting his mind race over all his memories, of the lessons that he learned in life, of tragedies experienced and roads that were meant to be walked down, but weren't, and roads that were walked down, but never should have been.

"It did have an effect," Darcy said, not strongly, but mystically. It was as if all the moments of his life had reached a place where he realized how he had come to be the man that he was. "I never thought of it before, Bingley. You know how you live your life and you just...continue on. You don't think or contemplate how you got there, but you just are there. And you soldier onward."

"Yes, I do know what that feels like."

"It's almost like that of a natural endurance; you continue on because you must. And so, you become this hard man, this strong and desperate creature, who must have the answers, or everyone else around you falls down. Because if they do fall apart, you feel as if it is your fault. Therefore, the first answer that anyone asks you must be the right one. You cannot falter or weaken, or the house of cards plummets down into a grave that you dug."

Darcy's eyes widened.

"My aunt blames herself for Anne dying."

"You think so?"

"Yes," he said, reaching a particular revelation that rendered him proud of himself. "Because that is the natural reaction that I would have."

When Lady Catherine was able to receive her guests properly, her black clothing would not hold her down. She came forward and started ruling Darcy's life as usual and making absurd suggestions to Mr. Bingley about renting out Netherfield Park. All of this was tolerated by both men, who sensed that the great lady just needed to find some balance in her life. And the surest way of doing so was by having someone to rule over.

Although Darcy might have withstood this for days upon end at another time of his life, he now had a fiancée in Milton, a friend who was in the throes of heartache, a cousin who wanted to marry his soon to be sister-in-law, a proper time to invite Georgiana to the North, and other problems that needed his attention. He could not remain as he wished...or could he?

At suppertime, Darcy decided to come up with his plan, but first he needed Lady Catherine to confront the pain that she was undergoing. That was the surest way he had of fulfilling his role as a nephew, a loving relative, while also remembering Elizabeth.

After supper, Darcy told Bingley to retire for the evening. Darcy would make an excuse that Bingley was feeling ill and that would give him the chance he needed to speak to his aunt in confidence.

"Ill?" Lady Catherine blurted out when Darcy gave this excuse. "Surely that cannot be correct. My cook gives a perfectly balanced meal. Something else must be ailing Mr. Bingley."

"That is most likely," Darcy dismissed immediately, "but it is of no matter. Aunt Catherine, since I have come, you haven't suggested that we visit Anne's grave."

When hearing this, Lady Catherine de Bourgh's skin changed color. It turned a whiter shade of pale and Darcy noted the difference. This was precisely how he wished to begin, and the best way was to attack the subject from the place that she held most dear.

"Aunt Catherine," Darcy said, "why have you never mentioned me paying a visit to her at all?"

Lady Catherine closed her eyes.

"You want to look at her grave. Very well, go and see it! Victor will show you the way."

"I would like it if you did. Aunt Catherine, something is wrong."

"Of course, something is wrong!" she spat out. "My baby is dead, Darcy, and you want me to go and see her, to remind myself? Who are you to lecture me?"

"You need to go and see her."

"Why?"

"Because you need to face this."

"I have faced it. I've been facing it for two weeks. I have gone to see her grave every day, and I cannot do it again."

"But you do not wish to show me?"

Lady Catherine looked away from him, and sat down, sitting in the position of a regal queen.

"And why is that?" Darcy asked. "Because there is something that you do not wish to face, but you must." Darcy sat down and took her hand in his again. "Aunt Catherine, what are you afraid of? You are sad because Anne is gone. But there is something else there, and you need to confront it."

"I don't need to confront anything."

"Yes, this is traditional heartbreak and anguish over losing one's child. When we are parents, we always plan to be the one to die first."

Lady Catherine began to weep slowly.

"It's not right, Darcy. I did everything. It's not fair!"

"Yes, you did do everything."

"No, I didn't. That's what I tell myself to ease the burden. I can't help but wonder what it is that I did, that makes me be punished now."

"You didn't do anything."

"Yes, I did. Perhaps I listened to the wrong apothecary, or she was given the wrong dosage. Or perhaps she should have been taken to town for the benefit of the newer doctors who have graduated at university."

"Aunt, listen to me. And look at me. Truly, look into my eyes." When she did, Darcy was adamant, determined to get her to listen to him. "You are blaming yourself, because of who you are. Ever since she was born, she was sickly, and you have been saving her from the fragile sides of herself. It reached a point where you had to dictate everything, to the point where you were the chief source of her life. As any mother ought to be. But you were not only that. You also were a wife to a knight. You had to run an estate. So much of your life was overseeing others. That has led to you feeling like you must put everyone's life in order, or chaos will follow. And when chaos does follow, you are confused. How could this have happened when you planned everything with such care?"

"Yes," Lady Catherine whispered, amazed that he understood her, "that's what I feel. I planned everything so perfectly."

Darcy sat down next to her.

"I did so once as well. I planned everything and it all fell apart around me. I was rejected, gave my friend wrong advice, and I suffered. And I asked myself, how could I have been so wrong? There were many answers to that, but one of them was simple. A wise person I once knew said 'when man makes plans, God laughs'." Lady Catherine chuckled sadly at this. "What that means, no matter what we do and how we do it, sometimes things are out of our hands. We can plan for the worst day, and still the rug is pulled out from underneath us. We can plan every aspect of our day, and once breakfast is over, the plan is already coming undone. You were a phenomenal mother. Anne knew this. Even when you smothered her with your affections, she appreciated it. You did everything to keep her alive for as long as you could. And you gave her the best chance. Wherever she is, she will always love you. She will always remember how you were the greatest mother she could have ever had. Aunt Catherine, her death is not your fault. God just decided to take her home."

"But why?" Lady Catherine asked. Standing up, she began to pace back and forth, naturally unsettled. Till now, all she had for company were servants. Her immediate family had all been either in the North or touring the continent. Therefore, when this terrible ordeal occurred, Lady Catherine had none of her own family to share her grief, lighten her woes—or even had to talk to. Now that Darcy was there, she could reveal everything. Her usual spirit of fortitude could not shield her now from the intensity of her emotions. "I am told that God has a purpose for all, but I don't see it here. I have no right to question him, but I cannot help it now. I am angry at whoever took my child from me. I want her back, Darcy. She was my life. She was my soul. I cannot live without my soul!"

"I know. And this has every right to hurt for a while. But I just don't want you to blame yourself. I don't want you hating yourself for choices that you didn't make, aunt. This was never your fault."

Sighing, she turned back to Darcy.

"I'm so sorry."

"For what? I told you that this was not your fault."

"No, not about that, but of other matters." Her face, surprisingly, looked repentant. Or rather, it looked ashamed.

Darcy never knew that his aunt was capable of shame. "I cursed you, nephew."

"Me?"

"Yes. I cursed you over these last few months. You think my eyes are blind, Darcy? But I have my contacts and know more than you have let on. I know that you went to the North to see Thornton."

"Well, it's no secret. I told the whole family that I was going to stay with my friend."

"Yes. But I also know that's where the Bennet sisters are."

With the conversation having taken a turn that Darcy did not expect, he confessed to being somewhat bewildered. How could she have known? Or moreover, why did she bring up such an incident now? What consequence could it matter?

"What of it?" Darcy asked. "They have a right to go where they wish and make a life for themselves. Especially with how callous your one-time reverend was in throwing them out of the only home that they ever had."

"It was his birthright."

"It was their home! Mr. Collins could have remained at Hunsford Parsonage when their parents died. But no, he chose to forget all the kind and generous words of the religion that he claimed to believe in so desperately, throw out five young women without connection or fortune to fend for themselves. Is that pious, madam? Is that the actions of a true man of God? No, it's not. And you know it. How would you have liked it if Anne had been removed from Rosings Park in such a manner? You would have come back from the dead and sought vengeance on whoever did that to her."

Darcy stood up and walked away, angry. Suddenly, a thought occurred to him. Turning around, he confronted his aunt.

"It was Mr. Collins, wasn't it? He's the one who wrote to you to tell you about where the Bennet family went."

Lady Catherine's unapologetic side presented itself as she responded proudly.

"And why should he not, pray? He was my clergyman, and when he inherited Longbourn, he naturally would be aware of where his cousins had ended up. One went to London for work, three of them got work in Milton, and the other got married to an officer. Naturally, I suspected that one of those adventurous geese would be Miss Elizabeth Bennet. Am I correct?"

"Yes. I saw her there often. We were much thrown in company together."

Aunt Catherine raised an eyebrow.

Darcy buckled under her gaze, not out of weakness, but out of consideration. He didn't wish to tell Lady Catherine of his plans just yet, for this was her moment of grief. It wasn't right to override that with his moments of happiness. Besides, he was intrigued about what his aunt had said before.

"You still haven't told me how you scorned me," he uttered, to get her to recall her previous confession.

"Yes," Lady Catherine said, "Darcy, you must forgive me. This was spoken out of grief."

"I am prepared for the truth. No truth has ever knocked me down, and no truth ever shall."

"This might."

"I believe that I am stronger than that."

"When...Anne left us all, I was angry. I told myself that if you had done your duty, came and married her when I willed it, then she would be here. I railed against you, thinking of paths that would never be walked down, that ought to have been. I told myself that I would never forgive you for it. That if you had married, my child would still be here with us."

Darcy was not upset, for he understood that it was spoken out of grief. However, he was unable to empathize with the lack of sense that her thoughts presented, even though they had come from a mind that had been filled with passionate sensibility that had been brought on by agony. Still, he was unable to resist asking.

"But Aunt Catherine," Darcy considered, "what would our alliance have done to prevent Anne's death? My marriage would not have saved her. In fact, there's the possibility that it would have ruined her. While it is... bewitching to marry for love, our alliance would have been of a peculiar kind. Since it had been forged when we were still infants, she nor I were given a say in the matter. If we did marry, she would be married to me out of obligation, and when she would become with child...Aunt, she would not have survived the delivery."

"But at least I would have had a grandchild to cherish!"

Darcy could not believe that she had said that.

"Do you hear yourself?" he cried. "Do you hear what you sound like right now?"

Lady Catherine looked away from him, stubbornly still as a statue.

"You would sacrifice your daughter for the sake of an heir."

"One thing matters above all: that Rosings Park has a de

Bourgh as an heir. Whatever my personal feelings, that is my right."

"Then why didn't you and Uncle de Bourgh have more than one child?" Darcy spat. "You wanted Anne to do her duty, then why didn't you do yours? You had one child, and that was it. Once it occurred to you that Anne was guaranteed to be sickly, you should have considered such. But you didn't. And why is that?"

"Don't talk nonsense at a time like this."

"No, let's talk nonsense," Darcy replied, angry. "Let's talk about the fact that you bore Anne because you viewed marriage to Uncle de Bourgh as a contract. Children were in that contract. You had one, so contract *fulfilled.* Anne wanted something else. She wanted to be with someone that she loved."

"And how do you know that?"

"Because Anne told me."

When hearing Darcy's exclamation, Lady Catherine barely batted an eye.

"I know," she responded, "she told me too."

Now Darcy was the one who was more surprised.

"I beg your pardon?"

"Your conversation with Anne about your future matrimonial misadventures made her brave. She thought she could approach me on the subject. She told me about how you talked. About how you both expressed a desire to marry elsewhere, to choose your own spouse. Apparently, you both agreed to find your happiness with some other person. Thinking she had your support, she came to me and told me about how you both were in agreement on the matter."

"She did?"

"Yes. But I put an end to all that really quickly. I ordered her to put that conversation right out of her mind. And I had meant to do the same to you as well, had you not gone running to see your tradesman friend in Milton."

"He's a manufacturer."

"Same meaningless position in society."

All sympathy had now been temporarily done away, all sense of respect for his aunt had been depleted, and he forgot that she was a grieving mother. He was so much offended, so terribly upset with her, that he thought it best to tell her the truth, the whole truth, and everything that it entailed.

"You bullied Anne, didn't you?"

"I made her see the right thing."

"You don't know what you have done. All the stress of knowing that she might have to marry me...distress can add to an illness. Sometimes the sickness does take hold of us, but a weak will can add to it." Darcy squinted, then suddenly, he felt a jolt of dread. It coursed through him, like a wave of dark energy. He didn't want to believe it—but it was possible.

No, it wasn't.

But yes, it was.

He could be very wrong.

But then again, he could be right.

There was nothing for it, but for him to press on and discover how right or wrong he was.

"That's why you hate yourself now, isn't it?" Darcy asked. The question was quite rhetorical because he didn't expect an answer.

Lady Catherine turned to him, her eyes like stone.

"You hate yourself, and blame yourself," Darcy continued, "because you realize that maybe you did drive her to despair. That maybe, by often desiring a match that she didn't want, you made Anne unhappy. By so doing, she became more out of spirits. Her sickly nature already had enough trials to bear, but now you added to those woes. Now you are scared. So very scared that your intentions might have driven her to her death."

"I will not stand and listen to this anymore. You are speaking nonsense."

Lady Catherine turned away from him and began to march out of the room.

Unwilling to lose the argument that he knew belonged to him, Darcy roared after her.

"I am right, aren't I? You walk away from me because you know that I am right."

Lady Catherine froze, but she didn't turn to face him. Her halted figure gave Darcy even more confirmation. If she disagreed, then she would have kept walking. But she stopped. She froze, and that was enough to signify that her true guilt had been discovered.

"You hate yourself now, because you realize that you were wrong," Darcy continued. "That you could have spent more time loving her, showing her all that life had in store for her, rather than making her cling to a future that she did not want. Now you are remembering all those times that you could have cherished with her, and how wasted they are."

Once more, Lady Catherine's figure began to slacken and regress. Realizing that he had made her face herself for long enough, Darcy knew that he had to put an end to this trial. The truth was laid plain. It was now a time for comforting.

"Whatever happened in the past," he said, softer, "you must not blame yourself for what could have been and should have been. Again, you did the best you could to give Anne the best life that you thought she deserved. Whatever my past, if Anne and I had married, I would never have mistreated her."

"I know. That's why I kept choosing you. Even when I knew that there was no hope of you both being in love. I knew, at least, my daughter would be safe under you."

"Yes. I am honored that you chose me, Aunt. But I was not the man for her. At least she avoided a fate where she was in a loveless match. Now she is free. Anne de Bourgh can go anywhere. She is free of her ill-health that held her back. She can fly anywhere and be what she always wanted."

"I want my child back."

"I know. Any mother would. Bingley and I will stay here till tomorrow to see that you are well. Then I must return. If you will be ready to take me to the grave, then I would be happy."

Not saying another word, Lady Catherine left him to make the arrangements for himself and Bingley.

Now that he was alone, Darcy breathed in a sharp breath and released it gradually.

He considered this to be one of the most difficult conversations in his life.

Little did he know...

Chapter 7

The Lucases Come to Milton

The next day, Margaret and Mr. Hale escorted me to the railway station in Milton. As we walked to the terminal that Charlotte and Maria Lucas would be arriving on, I confessed that I was a little nervous, and my worries were etched across my features.

"Why so unsettled?" Margaret asked me.

"I think you would get a shorter list of 'why should I not be unsettled'," I responded. "I have two friends who I am bringing to the North, an industrial town that is far away from anything that they know, I am asking them to become working-class, then I am asking them to live in conditions that would appear as squalid to their current domicile. Now that I am here, I wonder if maybe I had not thought my request through very well."

"Brave heart, Lizzy," Mr. Hale assured me. "When do we humans get anywhere without a little hope every now and again? Besides, if they come and do not like it, I am sure that we can find another way to resolve your situation."

"Father is right," Margaret assured me, "and Charlotte is

a very practical woman. I believe she knows how to maintain herself in such a place. But in case I am wrong..."

"Yes?"

"Well, if I am wrong, and they are critical of your live, then Lizzy, you might have to entertain the fact that they might not be the sort of friends that you want."

"That's what scares me as well. Is their friendship class-dependent? Then again, that's how we are raised to be."

"And now you know why I rushed to get to Hampshire when I did," Margaret said. "I wanted to find a better way." Out of the corner of her eye, she saw her father look uneasy at the mention of Hampshire. She took his arm to reassure him. "That was not discredit to you, but a mere implication for why I did not wish to remain in Harley Street. I had to get away from *that* sort of pretension. No more and no less." This eased Mr. Hale enough and soon we could turn our eyes to the oncoming train that was riding down the tracks.

The Lucases train had come in.

Mesmerizing!

That is the way that I define a train when it comes rolling in. For when it arrives and the people disembark, you wonder about them. Are they satisfied with their destination? Are they merely passing through? Are they here only out of obligation? Or are they here because they have no other choice? Is this the end of the world for them?

For what is Milton but a chain to some and a liberty to others?

What is any land but that?

Or maybe, every land is a bit of both. All we have to do is find one with the greater liberties and the lesser constraints.

The train came to a stop and soon the passengers exited the cars, to be met with friends and family—and then there were two.

From her light brown hair to her sister's blonde curls, I saw the familiar faces of Charlotte and Maria Lucas as they looked back and forth to search for where we were.

Maria had spotted us first. Smiling, she pinched Charlotte's arm to indicate where to look. Both sisters grinned and waved as we eagerly approached them. Moving my way through the crowd, I raced up to Charlotte, she opened her arms wide, and I fell into them. I felt the warmth of familiarity as we hugged and others moved away from us, giving us a wide berth.

"You came!" I laughed, seeing Margaret and Mr. Hale accost Maria Lucas, out of the corner of my eye and greet her warmly. "You really came!"

"Of course, I did," Charlotte said. "What? You sound as if I would leave you at the railway station, without anyone to meet. Give me credit, Lizzy."

"Yes, I know. I should not have been so anxious."

"Well," Charlotte Lucas said, as we released each other, but still held hands, "I am here, and I will not be the abandoning sort."

We both got a good look at each other. Charlotte may have been regarded as plain to some, but her sensible nature and her gentle smile naturally had a comforting effect that put everyone at ease.

"You are looking well," I said.

"That's a lie but thank you. You are looking stunning as always."

She turned to Mr. Hale and Margaret and kind words were spoken.

"Maria," I said, also taking her hand, "thank god you are come."

"Oh, this is marvelous!" Maria cried energetically. "Lizzy, what do you think? Riding on the train was such fun! I got to see the English landscape rush out before my very eyes. It is too long, too long, I tell you, since I had the privilege of being able to have an adventure. In Hertfordshire, we never get to go anywhere, so a diversion is always sought after. Now, so much I shall be able to tell. That's the thing about always being at home; there is never any news. And what are we humans without news? There must always be something to tell, of course."

"Maria, learn economy of words," Charlotte said, "you would make us look overzealous."

"Oh, do forgive me."

"There is no apology needed, I assure you," I said. "If you proved to be any less excited, I might think you didn't miss me, Maria."

"Well, let us get you to Crampton," Mr. Hale said, "you've had a long journey, and Mrs. Hale would want to see you."

"Do you still keep Dixon?" Maria asked, skipping merrily, excited from being in a new place.

"Oh, did we?" Margaret replied, "very much so. She wouldn't leave my mother even if she was forced to the ends of the earth."

"Good ole' Dixon," Charlotte Lucas responded.

Good ole' Dixon indeed!

"Miss Lucas and Miss Maria!" Dixon cried when we arrived at the Hale residence. "Well, as I live and breathe."

Dixon was all effusions of joy at seeing so many familiar faces. Truly, it brought her maternal side into even more prominence.

"It is good to see you, Dixon," Maria cried.

"Yes, and you girls are looking too thin for my liking. I'll bring you some shortbread and soon you'll be fattened up in a matter of weeks."

"Dixon, they do not even know if they will be staying," I pointed out.

"Yes, I've heard *that* before!" With that, Dixon went to the kitchen to begin preparing refreshments.

"Dixon cares for you," Mrs. Hale said, still looking a little sickly and holding on to her handkerchief while Margaret tended to her. "That's all. Take her fussing as the ultimate sign of endearment."

"We do, Mrs. Hale, I assure you," Charlotte said, but her tone was sympathetic, "I am sorry that you are not well. We must feel like a terrible imposition to you."

"None of that," Mrs. Hale responded. "In times like this, it helps to see more friends." She smiled sweetly at the Lucas sisters. "It is good to see you girls again."

"We are glad to have come, especially when there are such friends to be met."

"Still always saying the right thing," I teased Charlotte.

"You wouldn't like me any other way, and you know it."

"No, I would not."

"I know," Mr. Hale continued, "that when you become accustomed to Milton, you will find a novelty in it. I know that I have."

"You have an open mind that many of us wish to have, Mr. Hale," Charlotte continued, "but for the first time, I think I am wise enough to be similar. So far, from what I have seen of Milton, it is very different to what we are accustomed to. I admit, at the very least, I am curious about it."

"It is dirty here," Mrs. Hale said, "to be sure, never wear

white linens anywhere. But the activity is meant for the young, I suppose."

We all looked at her, sympathetic. We spoke on a little more, but when it became very evident that she was getting tired and company was the last thing she needed, I made an excuse that I wished to take the Lucases back to Frances Street before it got too late, and that was sufficient.

The Hales happily bid us farewell, offered to have us for dinner soon, and then we were off back to Princeton.

Due to their luggage, we had to take a carriage back to Princeton, but it was no matter.

"I asked Mr. Thornton if he would manage arranging a carriage for us at this time," I explained as their luggage was being assembled again and we prepared to wait for our transportation. "Mr. Thornton is a manufacturer and magistrate here in Milton Common."

When hearing this, Margaret gave me a subtle but swift look.

"I didn't know that he was arranging things," she observed.

"It was the best plan," I said, "when Darcy and Bingley left for Kent, he asked Thornton to tend to us if we should ever need him. I knew that we would need his help."

Margaret couldn't help but look flushed. Seeing her anxiety, I leaned in close and whispered in her ear.

"I do not do this to distress you. You know that."

"I know. But you'll make me quite ashamed of myself."

"Hush. Don't speak nonsense so early in the evening." I pinched her wrist gently to make her more comfortable. Her face slackened, she became at ease, and she was once again like herself.

When the carriage arrived—I was amazed at how I planned it all so perfectly, because it was around the time that Mrs. Hale could not endure too much more conversation—we all got in and were transported to Princeton.

When we arrived at Frances Street, the driver had to help us move the luggage from the main street to our house, because the carriage could not fit. We assisted him, thanking him for his service as I gave him a shilling. Of course, he would not accept it, which was no surprise. Even if he needed it, sometimes it felt inadmissible for a man to feel like a woman owed him for a common courtesy.

When Charlotte saw me help the driver carry her luggage, she did look on me in wonder, but soon, she adopted the 'when in Milton, do as the rest of Milton does' concept and she and Maria also carried the remainder of their things.

When the driver had departed, and we stood in front of our small house, Charlotte couldn't help but note the alteration.

"You've changed," she observed.

"No more servants to do everything for me," I replied, "you soon get used to becoming very independent in Milton. Or you don't. Depends on your spirit."

Finally, they looked at my dwelling.

"Yes," I said, taking in their expressions. "It's ghastly, I know. But when you see what my sisters did within, you will see that we have done our best to make it the most comfortable that we could."

"I'm sure you have," Charlotte responded, while Maria looked up and down Frances Street. It was a windy sort of road that was filled with the familiar gray aspect that most of Milton possessed. Charlotte was wearing a blue coat with a patterned dress underneath, while Maria was wearing a red one, and an elaborate bonnet. Both of them stuck out somewhat against the plain laboring clothing that the rest of the passersby wore when they saw us. From down the road, some of our neighbors waved to me, I waved back and began to unlock the door.

"Milton people are friendly enough," I explained, "so, they are more likely than not to be kind to you. But it's an industrial city, like any other, and there are some prickly sorts about."

"But what about on this street?" Maria asked. "Are there...villains here?"

What an important and impertinent question to ask. I knew better than to not answer it.

"There are villains everywhere, I have learned. However, when it comes to Frances Street, if you are kind to them, they are likely to be kind in return. But there are more fighters here than villains. There's a difference, and I wish I could explain it better. You'll see in time. No one here has the instinct to hurt you. It's not their way."

When we entered, it was to a delightful scene.

"Charlotte and Maria!" Kitty and Lydia cried, rushing up to them. Plato and Rasby were also in attendance. Maria and Charlotte were overcome by the affection that comes from meeting old friends.

When they met Plato and Rasby, it was just as those two were leaving, due to the hour. This was fortunate because the Lucas ladies were just newly come to Milton. Their first day being here was not the time to be come upon by new acquaintances. That's what tomorrow was for.

When they left, Lydia and Kitty began to press them with many questions while I went into the kitchen and began to prepare the food that I had planned to serve that evening.

"How is Hertfordshire?" Lydia asked.

"Is our Uncle Philips recovering from Aunt Philips's

death?" Kitty asked. "We are so very sorry. We wish that we could be there for him."

"We know it's been months now," Lydia said, "but Uncle Philips doesn't seem like the sort to recover from something like that."

"Some men are built that way, you know? One wife and that's the long and the short of it."

"And how is the dreadful Mr. Collins?"

"Is his wife as bad as him?"

"I wouldn't be surprised if she was. But if she is a nice woman, I feel sorry for her."

"Oh, please, Kitty! Of course, she is a horrid sort of creature. What kind and good woman would marry Mr. Collins?"

I smiled as all these questions were answered patiently, but with much affection on both sides. Maria and Charlotte were so happy to see us again that they were able to answer the questions cheerily.

"Mr. Philips is doing well," Charlotte said, "but I don't think it likely that he will ever recover from your aunt's passing. As you said, he really is a one-love sort of man."

"Makes sense," Lydia said, "besides, they were married for too long for him to even know how to live with another woman. He already found one who was accustomed to his ways and habits."

"In many ways, that's romantic," Maria said, "to be so devoted to the same woman that you cannot see your path with another."

"Sensible to some, and not so much to others," Charlotte responded. "But in Mr. Philips's case, I do believe that it is sensible."

"And what of Mr. and Mrs. Collins?" Kitty asked. "What of them?"

There was a distinct pause. This made my ears prick up, and I abandoned my spot and went to the doorway where I watched the sisters.

Filled with guilt and trepidation, I worried that I was going to see regret etched on Charlotte's features. That I was going to depict a woman who wished that she could go back and change the hands of time and unsay when she rejected Mr. Collins.

Thankfully, it was the contrary. Charlotte's silence was for another reason.

"One should not speak bitterly of anyone," Charlotte said, with a pained look in her eye, "but those two deserve each other."

"All their servants hate them," Maria interjected, without fear of sounding cold. "And my mother and father secretly always groan when we must pay our visit."

"He has a habit," Charlotte said, slowly, "of reminding me of what I missed out on when refusing him. He seems to speak in asides, or in a subtle manner, where he doesn't say such, but he means such. At first, my parents understood his vexation with me. But over time they have grown to see him for what he is, and they discover how much of a terrible fate that I escaped."

"And what of Longbourn?" Kitty asked. "Have they made alterations to it?"

"Lord, I hope not," Lydia scoffed, "it was perfect as it was."

"And it's the tendency of a newly made couple to always think things are not good enough for them," Charlotte responded. She looked at us heavily, sympathetic. "They have changed a few things in the sitting room."

I looked down at the thought of our home being altered in any way.

In many ways, I felt as if I was hearing a horrible story of a person getting galvanized, gutted from the inside out. Those were my sentiments when I heard of alterations being done to Longbourn. If I should ever return to Hertfordshire, what house would I be met with? After all, it may belong to the Collinses, but it would only be a matter of time before he would wish to invite us back—due to Mr. Collins's own ambitions. For, now that I was Mr. Darcy's fiancée, of Pemberley, and he was Lady Catherine's nephew, Mr. Collins would deem it in his best interests to enter our good graces. Things changed, and now there was something in it for him. Naturally, I would have no inclination to see him again, but his children would go on to be our family, and Hertfordshire was our home county. Seeing him again was inevitable and so was seeing Longbourn.

When hearing of the alterations that Charlotte described, Lydia and Kitty were fraught with despair and lamented that Mr. Collins would always be the most horrid creature in the world—after all, how dare he change our curtains?

Although, despite their hyperbolic speeches, I both understood and seconded their sentiments. Longbourn was the main constant in our lives. After all, despite one's wishes for their parents to always be alive, mama and papa were mortal. We should have known that we would lose them eventually, no matter what we told ourselves. But Longbourn was a building. It was a home, a strong home that tested and bested the elements time and time again. It was the equivalent to the Rocks of Stonehenge in our eyes, and so, it was immortal. It just felt right that a Bennet should always be there. So, here was where the boulder fell down the hardest.

After an hour of getting acquainted with the Lucas sisters, Denny came to retrieve Lydia and take her home. His eyes lifted when seeing Charlotte and Maria, and he felt the comfort of seeing old friends again. He invited them to come to the regiment's headquarters if they could spare an hour of their visit. The sisters agreed and Mr. and Mrs. Denny left just before I had finished making dinner.

Since Jane was staying at the Kirkpatricks' that evening, Kitty and I would share a bed, while Charlotte and Maria had Kitty's room. We showed them the rest of the house after dinner, and neither of us did anything to minimalize the smallness of our home. While the walls were painted well, and the house was well-decorated, it didn't change the fact that the house was a great deal lesser than Lucas Lodge. Maria and Charlotte were kind, however, and they complimented us on how well we had enhanced the house's appearance.

When they finished unpacking their things, I had their baths drawn, and Charlotte sat down with me while she arranged her hair into curling papers. We were in our nightgowns and found the comfort of speaking at our leisure—after all, we finally were alone in my room. Maria, younger and closer to Kitty's age, found a natural listener and more eager talker in Kitty. After all, her romance with Colonel Fitzwilliam was the sort of love story that would fascinate a girl like Maria Lucas.

"Well," I began, stoking the fire in the fireplace to heat up the room better, "you can be honest, dear friend. Now that we are alone, I can accept if you find it unappealing to live in such a place. I admit, the living conditions in Milton are quite ghastly."

"I will say no such thing," Charlotte said, rolling some more strands of her hair, "because it is not true. You know me very well, Lizzy. I believe in doing the best one can with what one has. You five inherited little to nothing, and you turned that into a fighting chance. This place is clearly a sign that you five will persevere until the end. Besides, you already have a legendary match." She turned to me, giggling. "Mr. Darcy, eh?"

I blushed.

"I know. I already was prepared to hear it."

"Yes, you had better have been!" she said, turning to me while she was still at her task. "I told you! Did I not? I told you that he admired you. But would you listen? No. It was always 'I hate him as much as he hates me' business. Or 'he has a propensity to relentlessly despise everyone' sort of talk. Mr. Darcy, the villain. Mr. Darcy, the cruel creature. And now you are in love with him. I would laugh if I wasn't so confused on how it all came about. But I am also happy. After all, marrying him is the most sensible thing to do."

"You think that I marry him out of sense as opposed to sensibility?" I asked, skeptical. "You cannot be serious. Did our discussion about Jane not showing more affection than she felt for Mr. Bingley until she loved him go heedless? Do you not think I would not apply that lesson to myself? I cannot marry a man who I despise."

"I know that you cannot. I know that you can afford to be romantic. I just add the fact that your match is sensible, because I prize when outcomes turn out in such a way for the benefit of one's affections as well as one's economy."

"I know," I replied, playfully rolling my eyes. "But yes, you were right."

"I liked hearing that in your letter to me, and I like hearing it now." Charlotte looked smug. "I cannot help but put my imagination to it all, though. If you had taken heed to my advice, and had married Mr. Darcy when you could, then Mr. Bingley's proposal to Jane might have soon followed. After all, you could have convinced Darcy that Jane really did love Bingley. Then you both would be married to both men, Kitty would have met Colonel Fitzwilliam sooner, and when your parents died, there would have been no need to come to Milton, and for Mary to work in your uncle's factory."

"Are you determined to make me feel guilty for arriving at my life's conclusions where I may?" I asked.

"Not at all. As much as it would have been better for you in the short span of things, I wonder now if maybe it had worked out for the best. You have been flung into a new world where you have learned how having a good life is not everyone's right, because they do not often have it. Sometimes, having a wider acquaintance with the ways of the world, you begin to appreciate things more. I believe that coming to Milton has taught you to appreciate every little bit of good fortune that comes your way. It taught you to look at life differently. Life becomes more beautiful when you are damned, doesn't it?"

Her words were like that of a heavy pair of boots: they were hard to carry with you, but they were necessary to have.

"Yes, I suppose life did take on a different hue. But through it all, Charlotte, when it comes to love, I still would have only chosen the best man for me."

"I know that you would have. And from a selfish place, your actions saved my life, therefore I owe you a debt."

What a surprise! Never did I see her speaking so.

"What inspired that sentence?" I asked.

"Well, if Jane had married Mr. Bingley, like I assumed would naturally happen, and then you had married Mr.

Darcy, like I believed could occur, then I would have possibly had no scruples in marrying Mr. Collins."

Every part of my body tingled at her confession—but the sensation was not out of satisfaction, but rather a perverse curiosity.

"Why? Where would that notion have its birth?"

"Well, I truly thought that Mr. Bingley would propose to Jane and that time would soften your heart to Mr. Darcy. After all, your mother talked about it so verbosely at the Netherfield Ball that we all expected a most advantageous marriage to occur very soon." She breathed in heavily, and her eyes were filled with a subtle guilt. "Now, I am not proud of this, you know. But sometimes, when a young lady is not born to a pretty face, she must find her fortune wherever she may. And I am a sensible woman, who has never really been romantic, nor could afford to be."

Quickly did I deduce what she meant.

"If Jane and I had secure futures and rich husbands, you would have accepted Mr. Collins's offer, wouldn't you?" I realized.

"Yes, I probably would have. After all, there would be no need to worry about you all being destitute, because you had married two exceedingly wealthy men. You both would have saved your family completely. Besides, if your father passed away, it would be traditional for the remainder of the family to move in with either you or Jane. Therefore, it would have hurt for you to lose Longbourn to Mr. Collins, but I think you would have forgiven me over time. And also, I would not have felt horrible for being its mistress. After all, you all had your happy endings. I would not be despised for wishing to have mine as well. Even if it wasn't so very happy."

I was about to brush my hair, but I was so enthralled

with what I was hearing that I held the brush midair, frozen in my place.

"Even if you were aware that you would not be happy being married to him?" I asked.

"Plain women must have something to live off of as well as the beautiful, Lizzy. Above all things, I will always have my instinct for self-preservation. Everyone does. And quite frankly, as long as it is not driven to excess, it is a good quality to have."

"But there is more to it," I said, folding my legs underneath me on the bed. "Because you sound different."

"It's because I am different. Or just better informed because time helped me. Yes, Lizzy, I would have married Mr. Collins, despite that neither he nor I loved the other, because it would be sensible. It would not have been something I felt guilt over because I knew your futures would be secure. But between Bingley not making Jane an offer, you not falling in love with Darcy, your futures were not secure. So, when Mr. Collins proposed to me, I was aware that I would take part in taking your future from you and I realized that I would be wrong for the rest of my life. And now I see that I have made my great escape. I would have regretted marrying him. Over time, his habits would have made me miserable, and the reward of being sensible would not be a good enough balm. However, if all went as I proposed, and I did marry him, then I would have sealed myself to such a fate. Ironically, it was your imbalanced future that saved me from making the largest mistake of my life."

I chuckled.

"So, our lives led to you not attaching yourself to a pernicious suitor. Well, I am glad that all our struggles saved something."

"Oh, I didn't mean to belittle your woes!"

"You weren't," I said, swiping the air dismissively, "I was just making a joke. But still, it is nice to be of service in a way. Whatever is the reason that you did not marry Mr. Collins, I am grateful."

"Thank you, Lizzy. I owe you much."

"Don't say that just yet. Remember? You have seen some parts of Milton. But you haven't seen all of it yet. You may hate me by tomorrow afternoon."

"I think not. I realized something about myself."

"And what is that?"

"That I grow weary of looking at the same drawing room. I think... I need an adventure of some kind. I need something new. Even if it is worse. As long as it is new. I think... I need perspective."

Chapter 8

And Then the Morning Comes

The next day came the beginning of Charlotte's new view on how her life would be. Kitty, Maria, Charlotte, and I ate breakfast, then Maria, Charlotte and I parted ways with Kitty.

On our way on the omnibus, Maria couldn't help but talk to me about something that I knew both fascinated her and scared her. In fact, I wouldn't be surprised if Charlotte was experiencing the same thing but simply was accustomed to not mentioning things that were unpleasant to talk about.

"Kitty told me how she and Raspberry became friends," Maria said, "I confess that I never would have foreseen such a development."

"Nor did I when I first came here," I acknowledged. Charlotte looked at me, still silent, but her eyes were hungry. I knew that I had been correct; she wanted to talk about Rasby and Plato but did not know how to approach the subject.

"You didn't?" Charlotte asked.

"No," I replied, unashamed, "for the first few seconds, I knew not what to think."

"So, the concept startled you as well?" Maria asked, equally as intent to know about my first reaction. I suppose, if they knew that I was as human as them, it would lessen their guilt. Oh well, we all must help where we may.

"My mind was thrown, and my judgment was askew," I elaborated. "Is that how you both felt?"

Maria and Charlotte looked at each other. Quite frankly, I wasn't in the mood to wait for them to reach a revelation about themselves when it was too late for them to do so.

"Come now," I pressed, "we don't have much time before we reach Granger Hall, and I have to introduce you to the professors. You didn't know how to talk to Raspberry or Plato, did you? You didn't know what to make of them, nor did you understand why we talk to them?"

"Well," Charlotte began, "we believe in their freedom, of course."

"I know. But being told to treat someone equally is strictly academic, until you meet them. It's not your fault; we were raised in situations that were so far removed from experiences that you are undergoing now, that you are not prepared. Well, it's time to become so."

"I just...don't know how to approach them," Maria said, "Kitty discussed it all with me last night. So, I know I was wrong on how I first viewed them. But..."

"It does change the fact that we were trained to think ourselves superior."

"Well," Charlotte began, "aren't we?"

I was unsurprised at her remark. It was a popular theory to be impartial, but not actually practice it. It is the way of the world to talk prettily, to hide the fact that none of us are aware that we have fallen into the fishpond.

"What I mean is—" Charlotte began, her words rushing out to hide that she realized how she sounded.

"I know what you mean," I began, "it's better to confess that you feel this way now. You can release it from your conscious and subconscious. You know that all are equal, but you have been trained to believe that we know best and that we can enlighten others? It's natural. That is what we have been taught. I was often the same way. However, we were given good lessons but left to practice them in pride and conceit. We are better than no one. And as for Plato and Rasby, don't go into discussion with them with preconceived notions. Don't go into your actions mimicking how others view them. And don't be afraid. That's the worst thing you can do. Mistakes have been made against them because of our fear of something so wholly different being presented to us. That tendency will always be humanity's great mistake, I suppose. The fear of the unknown. Well, now you do know them, and that is the choice you must make now: rule your conversations with them through fear...or confront the reality that you can just be around them and enjoy a different experience. But remember this: the first step to treating people equally is to accept that you once viewed them as unequal. The second step is to accept that defect of your character, and that it is a defect that might *always* be there. Once you acknowledge it, it no longer has any power over you. You need to acknowledge its existence, because if you don't, it will devour you. Prejudice is like any beast: feed the beast, or it feeds on you."

Charlotte and Maria looked between each other. At first, they remained in their seats, contemplating what I had said.

"I asked Kitty how she overcame it," Maria commented.

"Really?" I asked. "And what did she say?"

"It made me ashamed of myself when she did."

"What was it?" Charlotte stressed.

"She said that she saw the difference between she and

Raspberry for about five minutes, and then she just forgot about it. It was like she just didn't care."

My eyes widened.

"She said it better than I did, and in shorter sentences," I joked, "now I feel humbled."

Charlotte opened her mouth and closed it again.

"Speak now or forever hold your peace," I suggested, to encourage her to let out whatever was on her mind. "Remember, it's life and life only."

"I always viewed myself as being sensible," Charlotte inferred. "Perhaps I may have prided myself on that."

"You are sensible."

"Then why is this difficult for me?"

"Because it just is. Accepting it is the first step."

"I worry...that I might never be comfortable."

"You are young, you buffoon. You have the rest of your life for time to help you grow and get over yourself, don't you think?"

My last comment lightened her mood.

The poor woman: she was not used to being wrong and gruesome. That was another habit of mine where I had more experience than she did.

We arrived at Granger Hall and soon were met by Mr. Honnicut.

"Ah, which one is to be your replacement?" he asked merrily.

"Miss Charlotte Lucas, of Lucas Lodge. This is her younger sister, Miss Maria Lucas."

They curtsied as he offered his hand to shake.

"Oh, dear," I sighed, "I forgot to teach you the custom of Northern habit."

Charlotte and Maria blushed, insecure.

"No matter, no matter, no matter," Mr. Honnicut said, bowing to them, "I can adapt to Southern styles of things every now and again."

"Thank you, sir," Charlotte responded, "however, I do wish to have the gift of learning quickly, so let us begin now."

Charlotte offered her hand to shake, and Mr. Honnicut took it.

"First lesson in this place," she inferred, "learn to adapt."

"Well, that principle will help you go far here. In Milton, the speed of life is undoubtedly faster-paced than in the South. Any attempt to match that speed will help you."

"I am not afraid of being given advice."

Mr. Honnicut looked at me.

"I might like her almost as much as yourself."

"She has more sense than I," I complimented Charlotte.

"We shall see. Now, my class is first, Miss Lucas and Miss Maria. I gather that you will sit in with Miss Bennet and shadow her notetaking skills?"

"I will," Charlotte responded, "but I wish for you to know that I have mastered shorthand, and I will apply my skills to the test if I find that I am sufficient for the purpose."

"You seem apt enough. Good luck, my dear."

Out of the corner of my eye, I spied someone watching us. Turning, I saw Mr. Hanley watching us from a nearby doorway. Smiling, I was about to open my mouth to introduce him, but he only smiled slightly at me, retreated into the room, and closed the door behind him. Dismayed by this, I threw myself into my current task.

Retrieving my desk, pen and paper, Mr. Honnicut escorted us to the lecture hall. Soon, his students began to file into the class, and they spied Charlotte and Maria sitting beside me.

While Charlotte might still be regarded as plain, Maria was a fairer sort. Yet, each one of them had novelty on their side, so the men couldn't help but take notice of them.

Their blatant stares were enough to make Maria blush, but Charlotte was more aware that she might not have been as admired as Maria, therefore, she tended to the lecture immediately and watched me as I began to take notes.

The class went splendidly, and Mr. Honnicut was soon to become Charlotte's favorite speaker so far. This made proper sense, because he was the kindest of the professors, excluding Mr. Hale. Also, his general, kind nature and good cheer was not marred by a façade and false presentation. You did not have to worry of him praising you to your face and ridiculing you behind your back. His good nature was brought to you when you were facing him and lingered when your back was turned.

After Mr. Honnicut's class, I gave Charlotte my notes, to see how efficient she was at copying them. While she did so, Mr. Honnicut sat with Maria and I, eagerly inquiring about Maria's life. I was not the only lady from the South who had fallen into his life, and he was taking advantage of the experience.

Maria asked him every question she could, and her eagerness was so innocent that Mr. Honnicut was flattered by it.

After Charlotte finished copying two pages of my notes, I compared them to my original and it was nice to see that her handwriting was clear, and she copied my words accurately. Mr. Honnicut praised her handwriting, and if she was interested, then he was willing to have her come the next day and attempt to copy notes for the next class. If she could master the speed, then he would rule her as an adequate substitute.

"Not a superior substitute, mind you," Mr. Honnicut said, flattering me, "but an adequate one will suffice. However, Miss Lucas, you have to bear in mind that I am not the only professor that you have to please." He turned to me. "Mr. Dennison has an afternoon session, doesn't he?"

"Yes," a voice came from our left, "I do."

We turned, and Mr. Dennison was standing in the doorway.

"Yes, I do indeed."

Oh, good lord!

Mr. Dennison just had to be the professor that day.

Rolling my eyes, I grimaced as I faced him.

"Well, look what the devil dragged in," I commented, "his squalid spawn."

"You are one to talk, succubus."

"Whatever are your feelings for me, kindly don't take it out on my friends."

"Are they your friends?"

"Yes, they are."

"And, as I understand it, one of them seeks to replace your post while you go off and marry a rich man."

"I marry a worthy man, and yes, you worthless pile of horse excretion."

"Then your friend is guilty by association."

"Dennison," Honnicut said, "be neither a dunce, nor a

viper. If you are not going to be pleasant to these ladies, then you may shift for yourself and ignore them altogether. I'm not in the mood to suffer you to pass."

"I walk where I wish and speak to whom I shall," Dennison responded.

"Then why remain alongside people that you do not like?" I asked, trying to poke a hole in his logic.

"Very well," Dennison replied, "for the first time since you arrived, I knew that you would bring chaos in your wake. And how right I was."

"Don't walk away bitter," I advised, "just walk away."

"I walk away now, not because you told me to, but because it would suit my interests."

Turning his heel, he walked to his office.

We turned to Maria and Charlotte, who looked astonished.

"If you should come to work here," Mr. Honnicut explained to Charlotte, "time will make you accustomed to him."

"You mean that he improves on further acquaintance."

"God no," both Mr. Honnicut and I said together. Our speaking in unison made us all chuckle.

The next class to record was Mr. Dennison's.

"Oh dear," Charlotte whispered to me, "he is actually a good speaker. I was hoping he would be terrible."

"So did I when I first took notes for his class," I whispered back, barely moving my lips. "Sometimes, life is just not fair on who it distributes talent to."

"Yes. It is a shame."

Mr. Dennison proved that talent and tact sometimes worked

in inverse proportions. Every now and again, why did the most talented people in the world also have to be the most unlikeable? The answer was simple, of course: they were human.

When the class ended, Mr. Dennison's class clapped for him, despite that they didn't like him either, and he arranged his books as they left. After finally packing everything away, he snapped his suitcase closed, walked down the aisle, and slowed down as he neared us.

He turned to us, with a sharp glare, and I returned it proudly.

"I want my notes perfect. Well, as perfect as *you are able*."

"Mr. Dennison," I inferred, "eat dirt and die."

Saying no more, he stomped out of the hall and prepared to leave for the day.

I turned back to Charlotte.

"The trick is to show no fear. Milton will respect you for that."

"How did he get like that?" Charlotte asked. "Or is it just a general prejudice to female employees?"

"Oh, make no mistake. It's directed at us. But there's more to it than just general prejudice. Some time, a long time ago in his own history, Dennison had his heart broken. He's hated women for it ever since."

"Truly?"

"Some people use love like a weapon of venom. Dennison is one of those. Purgatory hath no constant torment like a man scorned. And that's compiled with all the cruel lessons that the world teaches them about us. Do not let his words shake your resolve."

"Another thing I have to grow accustomed to," Charlotte realized. "I admit, I'm not used to being disrespected."

I couldn't help but be a little vindictive.

"Rasby and Plato understand that predicament."

Charlotte understood the magnitude of my reference. In this wide world, we all have something in common: we have all been the victim of a bully at one time or another.

The workday was finished, and we rode the omnibus back to Princeton.

When we arrived home, it was to see Jane returned to us from visiting the Kirkpatricks home. She wasn't alone, again. Rasby, Kitty, and Plato were there, and they had a surprise for us.

"We made dinner," Kitty said, "to celebrate your visit to Milton and to give Lizzy a day off from cooking."

"Oh, thank god for that," I sighed, relieved. "I had no desire to cook anything. But I'm also hungry."

"Charlotte and Maria!" Jane cried, rushing up to them. "You have found us."

"Yes, we did," Maria cried, rushing into her embrace. "Oh, to see the world that you have woken up in."

"I know that Milton doesn't have much appeal upon first visiting," Jane said, still holding Maria's arms, "but this is the one time that I will implore anything of you. Do not be frightened by the smoke, or the strange new faces, or by the foreign feeling of it all. Give it a chance. Maria, please do this, for me."

Maria was truly humbled by Jane's immediate plea, for she was not accustomed to Jane ever being urgent in any sort of request. In fact, I do not even think that Maria was used to Jane even speaking that quickly. The mark of change that the

North usually brings, showed all over Jane's countenance and visage.

Maria's surprise at the immediate appeal was evident, by her expression, and Jane realized that she was being too forward.

"Oh dear, look at me," Jane acknowledged, humbled, "here I am, and what a display! You have only just walked through the door, and I immediately start asking things of you. For shame, I daresay, against myself."

"Not at all," was all that Maria could say, "It only shows me that you do need my help, and that is different than the usual way of things. No one ever needs my help at anything back home. It is just a change. That is all. But it's a welcome change." Maria looked at Jane and took in her augmented beauty. "I can see that you really are happy, and that Mr. Bingley finally came around to the purpose we expected him to arrive at after the Netherfield Ball."

"There were nights I sat up, cursing Bingley because he didn't get to the point," Kitty said to Rasby, "but over time, I was happy he didn't, and it took so long."

"Why?" Charlotte asked. "I do not ask to correct you, but out of curiosity."

"Because, if he had arrived at the right conclusion when he did, we would have never had to come to the North. And I don't care what everyone says, our family needed the change."

"Do you think so?" Plato asked.

"Yes. We had grown too complacent, if you ask me. Too much not appreciating what we had, until everything was taken from us. Then we had no choice but to grow up and find out who we were. None of us fell into despair, shriveled up and became a leaf among other people's plans. We kept going. If we had never been forced to learn independence, we would not be here now. And I do not apologize, but I like where we ended up. I daresay it would not have been more interesting if we simply followed the path that was expected of us in the South."

"It is a fact," Rasby noted, "that a young lady ought to have one great journey in her, and if she can't find it in her village, then she had best do it somewhere that she can. I know that's what I did, come what may."

"Precisely. I know that I wasn't meant to sit still and do nothing for the rest of my life," Kitty said, "here, I felt like I did something. And it's mine. No one can touch it. I couldn't say that if Jane had married Bingley and Lizzy had married Darcy too early. I don't think I was ready to amount to much. In short, if it all had ended differently, I don't think that I would have had a delightful time. As selfish as that may sound. Then again, I have never pretended to be a saint, nor aspire to a sainthood that others would thrust upon me."

"But all the horrors that you all suffered," Maria noted, "what of them? Surely you do not cherish those."

"If we didn't recover, perhaps those would be worth regret," Rasby inferred, "but we did recover, so it was just another incident that we had to rise above."

"It shouldn't have happened," I added, "but it did. We can't change that, so we just let it be another chapter that's among others. Sorry, I just gave up regret long ago. Endurance becomes more of your specialty when you have survived something. Besides, Plato was there to look after us, along with Darcy."

"Ah yes," Charlotte said, turning to Plato, "I remember now that you did the deed in saving my friends. I have been remiss in my thanks."

"No thanks are required," Plato said, charmingly and without any awkwardness that comes from rejecting gratitude. As we removed our outerwear, he was setting the table with Kitty and Rasby. "I'm an officer. Saving women had best be in the description, or what else am I? Much must be done, for a lady's happiness. I hope you and Miss Maria like beef, potatoes and salad."

"We do," Maria said.

"Good, because that's what my sister made."

"I helped!" Kitty said, pinching Plato's arm.

"Ouch," Plato responded.

We all sat down to eat.

Throughout the meal, Jane told Maria all about the Kirkpatrick children and about little Molly Gibson.

Hearing about little Molly's name sent a sharp sliver down my spine. When hearing of the niece, I was reminded of her uncle. I still had not approached Mr. Hanley about his heart, and I knew that it was something that I ought to do. I suppose...maybe I was frightened at the prospect. After all, I could be presumptive. Maybe Mr. Hale was wrong. Maybe he didn't want to talk about it. But perhaps Hanley needed a closure that only conversation could give. All that I could say is that no one who does not care for the feelings of others, never seeks to break anyone's heart. It is not a diverting activity. I didn't want to hurt Hanley. But no matter what I did, or how I did it, I had to hurt him. It, perhaps, might be the only way for him to move on.

When the dinner ended, Plato and Rasby took their leave. We did the washing up and prepared for bed. I went to my room, where I knew Charlotte was eager to discuss the day with me. As I did, I accidentally overheard Maria and Kitty talking.

"Kitty," Maria said, "I cannot help it. I feel so evil. I do not think that I will ever fully be comfortable around Rasby and Plato."

"It's natural to think that way, every now and again. You've been forced to think so. But do not expect me to ever abandon them. It's not in my nature. You'll find your courage one day, Maria. I suppose I have more experience of falling down on my face than you do. You don't have the experience of suffering under moral mishaps. Well, I do, and I don't walk the halls weeping over it. I confront it. You are not used to having a dangerous flaw. Now you do, and it scares you. You will overcome it, eventually. Then you will slip again. And you will have to try all over again. But until then, welcome to being human."

Ah, Kitty.

She was a creature who sometimes I would not give enough credit. But that is the problem with organic and unrewarded virtue: it never gets praised. It just gets expected.

But whoever knows if that is the wrong thing? After all, if good behavior becomes something that gets praised, rather than it being something that is simply expected, then people will begin to do it solely for the praise. And goodness becomes an act of vanity as opposed to an act of selflessness. But if we do not get praised for our good deeds, then it can signify that we do not appreciate virtue.

But where do good deeds done out of general nature begin and good deeds done out of vanity end? I'm sure that I do not know. Oh, I have a headache. Long ago, I promised myself never to philosophize so late at night. It didn't bode well for a tranquil slumber. When did I forget that maxim?

Sometimes, I wish I was an idiot and content to be so. Those sorts always sleep well.

Oh well, whoever said life was easy?

Chapter 9

What Must Be Done Cannot Be Done Too Quickly

That same morning, Darcy had woken up to a feeling of confusion. Despite all that had occurred between him and his aunt the day before, he wondered that he even found the means to sleep at all. For when one's mind is full, there is little room for peace in slumber. However, he was well refreshed, and therefore he was prepared to face what may come—or not come.

One of Lady Catherine's valets assisted in dressing him, and he went to Bingley's guestroom to see if he was awake. Bingley was in the process of getting dressed when Darcy retrieved him.

"How does your aunt do?" Bingley asked as the valet placed his waistcoat on him.

"She is grieving," Darcy said, unwilling to be more intimate while a servant was with them. "Everything she says is natural for her situation. She needs time—then again, I wonder if even that would help. Bingley, imagine what it would feel like to lose a child?"

"Not just a child, mate. But your *only* child. It probably feels worse than dying."

"Because it is," the valet said to their utter surprise. After he spoke, the valet immediately apologized for interrupting.

After a moment's pause, Darcy was curious.

"Do you speak from a place of understanding, Hopkins?" Darcy asked. "Have you ever lost a child?"

Hopkins, the valet, was surprised that Mr. Darcy asked him such a thing. After all, Darcy had never inquired after his family before.

"Yes, sir," Hopkins responded, a little strained, "my first-born. She was five years old. She was taken by fever."

"I'm sorry."

"Thank you. Time has helped me recover from it, but I can never forget, you see?" Hopkins tied Bingley's cravat. "I suppose no proper father could. You spend months wondering what you could have done to prevent it. It wasn't until half a year after the event that I had to accept that there was nothing I could do. Sometimes, time deals you sorrow instead of mercy. But then you train yourself to move on. That's what Lady Catherine will do. She is a strong woman. You know your aunt. She will recover. But it is a wound that she will carry with her for the rest of her life."

Hopkins finished dressing Bingley, and both men left Hopkins to himself, to go down to breakfast. Little did they know, that once they were gone, Hopkins sat down, forlorn, remembering his lost child, Henrietta, who he knew would have grown up to be a fine young woman.

When the gentlemen went down to breakfast, Lady Catherine was already there to be the perfect hostess. Her face was as proud and unaffected as ever, and one would not have suspected that she had spent the day before in torment.

Darcy and Bingley greeted her politely, but a little uneasily, and they all sat down.

"You both looked as if someone had killed your favorite hunting hound," Lady Catherine noted, observing them as they were eating. "When last I looked, I was the one who was supposed to be allowed to be forlorn."

"Forgive us," Darcy responded gently, "we just didn't know how to approach you this morning. It is a delicate business, you understand."

"Yes," Lady Catherine responded, her tone becoming gentler, "thank you for considering that. However, whatever I am feeling will not overtake me so far that I forget how to be a hostess. No, let that never be said of myself, for I pride myself on my ability to withstand a great deal. I daresay that there are few people who can recover, while still grieving, in a manner such as I can. It is a quality of my character that I take the most reverence in."

Seeing Lady Catherine returned to her usual boasting nature made Darcy feel that there was a sense of hope on the horizon for her. She was still in mourning, but this was a sign that his aunt, the Great Lady Catherine de Bourgh, would find her way back to the world that she ruled over so much.

"Darcy and Mr. Bingley," Lady Catherine said after a few bites, "since it is very fine out, you both ought to accompany me to see my poor Anne, and where she rests. I shall soon make it my habit to make sure there are fresh flowers on her grave for the rest of her life. If you would oblige me?"

"Yes," Darcy answered, "of course, Aunt."

"Very good. Now, both of you arrived in a carriage. That is good of you. I do not trust always riding around on railroads. There is something so very unsavory about the sight of tracks along the English countryside. It ruins the aesthetic and if I was running this country, I would put a stop to such industry. Especially the amount of factories in the North. No, many a picturesque setting has been ruined by the image of smoke across a sky."

Lady Catherine continued to talk on in this presumptive manner. For the first time in his life, Darcy welcomed it. And perhaps so did Bingley.

With some people, a return of their haughtier and prouder side was an indication that they were recovering, and for some reason, that was the light that you could hope for. A flawed family member was easier to respond to as opposed to a broken one.

After breakfast, they went to Hunsford church. Since the parsonage was not that far from it, the parson waddled out of his home and greeted the three of them most eagerly.

'Oh, my word!' Darcy groaned inwardly, 'my aunt found another version of Mr. Collins. Where does she find these odious religious caricatures?'

Darcy's first impression proved to be accurate. This new reverend had a tendency to bob up and down at Lady Catherine like he was a duck who was seeking approval at every turn. From one perspective, he was just trying to please his patroness, which was admirable. But since it made him look like a fool in the process, Darcy didn't have much patience with him.

The reverend led them to the church's cemetery, and eventually, they came upon Anne de Bourgh's grave. When seeing it, it brought the reality of Anne's departure from the earth fully to its apex, and Darcy found himself unsettled.

"Poor woman," Bingley uttered. "She was so young. It was wrong."

"Thank you, Mr. Bingley," Lady Catherine de Bourgh replied, "she was." She folded her hands in front of her, still as a statue. Except for her eyes. Within them was a dread, sadness, and quiet but dignified alarm. Tears were swelling up within them, but she was doing everything to restrain them.

Darcy walked up to the grave, bent down next to the headstone, and ran his hand down it.

Behind him, he heard his aunt gasp and cover her mouth.

"Have I upset you by doing that?" Darcy asked her. "I meant no harm by it."

"I do not shudder from careless offense, nephew. It is only...that's what I did when I first visited her. Her headstone was the only thing that could be touched."

"It's all we have left, I suppose." Darcy turned back to the headstone and began to talk to it, as if he was speaking to Anne herself. "You and I were born to a fate that terrified us. It led to us dreading each other's company. But in the few times, in the little bit of times that you and I could be kind to each other, we did. I do not forget those moments, however fleeting those moments were. I do not forget the one time where you wore a gown that you detested, due to its vulgar and ostentatious appearance. You looked at me, grimaced and showed all your disgust in a quiet way. It made me laugh. But now that I am here, and now that I see you, I realize that we didn't have enough of those times. God takes when he will, and we are not to question. But I do regret that you were just beginning to reach your womanhood—and you never got the chance to have it. But wherever you are, now you can be free. Now you can go where you will, be the woman that you wanted, be free of sickness and earthly woes. Go to the skies, Anne, and see everything that a woman ought to see. Sooner or later, we shall find you again."

Behind him, he heard it but was dignified enough not to look: Lady Catherine was crying in earnest.

At first, he let her do so.

Suddenly, seized by an urge to care for her, he walked up to her and hugged her tightly. She fell into his embrace and nephew comforted aunt.

When they finished, they returned to Rosings Park. When Bingley and Darcy had a moment to speak between themselves, Darcy noticed Bingley's agitated state immediately.

"You miss Jane, don't you?"

"It's not only that, Darcy, but it's the anxiety of it all. At this point, Maria Lucas will have come to Milton. What if she does not like it there? What if she rejects Jane's position? The Kirkpatrick family will not just want any new governess to take charge of their children. And then there is little Molly Gibson to think about."

"If she doesn't choose to take Jane's place, then Thornton will help me make inquiries and get a replacement as soon as possible. This is one of the few times that I embrace optimism for us."

"I'm usually the pleasant one."

"But I'm the one in love with Jane's younger sister. No doubt Elizabeth's influence has worn on me a little."

"We are marrying sisters." Bingley grinned. "Oh forgive me, I shouldn't be merry now."

"It makes sense. When you encounter death, your first instinct is to cling to life. I'm also excited, until I think of another prospect on the horizon."

"What prospect?"

"Bingley, how can I tell my aunt, who just lost her daughter, that I wish to marry a whole other woman soon?"

Bingley's eyes grew large at the prospect of facing such a task.

"Oh. Oh, my word. I am glad I am not you, at present."

Darcy rolled his eyes.

"Thank you for your support."

When it was time to dine for supper, Darcy dressed and still was planning his strategy on how he was going to tell his aunt about Elizabeth. He thought it best to first begin with the subject of his departure and then mention it. If the moment did not seem right, he would feel the cowardice of his actions...and just return to Milton and send Aunt Catherine a letter. But that was the last resort that he wished to do.

Going down to dinner with Bingley, Lady Catherine wore her finest black gown.

"Well, tomorrow, we shall visit the neighbors so that you both can make a traditional reintroduction into the village," Lady Catherine instructed. "The Heralds and the Prestons will be glad to see you both."

When hearing of the lengthy visit that Lady Catherine had anticipated, Darcy and Bingley looked at each other, shocked. They had no idea that she entertained the idea of them staying with her. However, soon Darcy realized that he should have anticipated this action. Of course, she would want them to stay, and of course she would order their lives. What was a poor nephew to do but have to hurt his aunt at the time where she needed him most?

"Aunt," Darcy said, "I do not mean to disoblige you. You know that. But Bingley and I must journey back to Milton tomorrow morning."

"Why, pray?" Lady Catherine declared. "What pressing business must you have there? This friend of yours, Thornton, is a tradesman."

"A manufacturer."

"Those are the same thing. What brings you to befriend such men, I have no notion. You are not raised to associate with those of trade. There is nothing for you there. And I do not see what would take you away from your aunt that you leave me at a time like this?"

Darcy looked at his plate, a little ashamed. Whatever his pride was, she was still his aunt, and he did feel familial ties to her.

"Right at the time where I need you most," Lady Catherine said. "Darcy..."

"I do care for you, aunt."

"Then show it, for heaven's sake! Look at me. I have an empty home, my daughter and heir has left me, and I need to make more arrangements. How can you abandon me so?"

Darcy's guilt would only go so far, but it did not need to be strained. For, deeper than his emotions was his intellect and his ability to connect a tragedy with a happy future. Heir? Rosings Park was now without an heir! And he knew just where to find it, and where to patch up Lady Catherine's broken heart.

"Aunt," he said, with a slight eagerness in his voice, "there is more to Milton than just my own interests. There is something there to interest you as well."

"And what would that be?"

"Your new heir. A nephew of yours who was born unfortunate, who you can now save from the destitute life that he was given. And this way, as you lose a daughter, you can gain a son by him. Aunt Catherine, there's Colonel Fitzwilliam. Make Richard your heir!"

When hearing that, Lady Catherine's whole countenance shifted. She went from a desperate woman who concealed it with dictatorial pride, to one of intense interest.

"Richard!" she repeated. "Dear Richard."

"Yes. You love him so much, Aunt. How often you have boasted of him being very attached to Rosings, and he is. Colonel Fitzwilliam is the precise sort of man that can run Rosings while being devoted to you as the main authority of the home. Adopt him as your heir, and Rosings and the family will be saved."

Stricken by the thought of Colonel Fitzwilliam, one of her favorite nephews being the heir to her home, made her drop her fork. She sat there, imagining the possibilities. Bingley and Darcy looked at each other, wondering what she was thinking.

At last, she looked between them both.

"Colonel Fitzwilliam has always shown a love for the estate, and he is the sort who knows not to be frivolous, because he is used to being economical. And he is a good and steady sort of man. I always wanted a son."

Suddenly, she stood up, walked over to the window, and peered out of it.

"I want it to be rightly understood," she declared, "that no one can take the place of my daughter. Nothing ever will."

"I understand that," Darcy assured her.

"Yes," Bingley said, a little uneasy since he was worried that he would sound presumptuous by talking. "Of course, you were a devoted mother."

"But before anything else, I must think of Rosings Park," Lady Catherine stated, "for it is *another* child of mine. It must always remain in the family, and I will see to it that it must go to the best hands for when I...am gone."

"You are healthy."

"But I am not young, and Anne's departure from our lives has reminded me of how mortal we all can be. When you are young, you feel as if you will never die. And then the young do die, and we elders feel it even more keenly. So, this must be set down and remembered! I love Anne more than anything, and nothing shall replace her in my heart. But for the love of Rosings and for the love of family—yes, you all mean a great deal to me—I have always been proud of the Colonel. He has shown himself to be a steady and reliable man. He is kind, but firm when he needs to be. He is responsible and understands great estates of extensive grounds. His joint guardianship of Georgiana displays that he is dependable. If you could not be the master of Rosings, he is without doubt, the next best choice. And with me being here, I can advise him on how to run everything. He would be here with me often. I would have company. I should prefer that more than anything."

She turned back to them, animation back in her face.

"Yes, I will write to my brother about the matter, and it will all be made final. Colonel Fitzwilliam will be my new heir of Rosings Park."

When seeing that his notion was so well-received, Darcy now saw his chance.

"Aunt, this is wonderful, and I am sure that you have it in you to make all the preparations as soon as possible. After all, what ought to be done cannot be done too quickly. But there is another matter which might either bring you a stressful situation, or it may bring you joy. Colonel Fitzwilliam is engaged to be married to a young woman who is worthy of him. The reason they have not married is due to their financial situation."

"Is this woman poor? Surely, she cannot be worthy of him."

"But she is. She was born to landed gentry. She is a Miss Catherine Bennet. Elizabeth Bennet's little sister."

Lady Catherine chuckled sardonically.

"Truly?"

"Yes. She was living comfortably until their parents died. That must be remembered."

"I know. Oh, that explains it all even more now. You've been visiting Thornton as well as watching Colonel Fitzwilliam as he entered into this courtship. Well now that he is my heir, he can do better."

"Aunt, he does not want to. She is his perfect match. I have seen it with my two eyes. Also, by marrying her, he might save her from destitution. And so would you."

"And her sisters too, no doubt."

"And you could plan their wedding."

When hearing that, Lady Catherine's eyes lit up in surprise.

"Aunt, you will not only have a son, but you will also have a daughter-in-law who will need all the help in the world when it comes to running a household. In fact, Kitty is the sort who might even prefer you to still organize every-thing while she is content just to be married to Richard."

With every word spoken, Lady Catherine's mind danced at the possibilities. She could plan a wedding as well as have a male heir who she knew she could dictate over without him feeling offended. When having faced death alone for so long, she was excited for new life to be brought to Rosings Park.

"Very well. Miss Elizabeth Bennet proved to be a unique

sort of creature. I'm sure that I can grow to tolerate a sister. But I must meet her first before I approve of her."

Any sort of affirmation was encouragement for Darcy, and now it came time for him to add the final weight that could either make or break everything.

"Well, there is more news," Darcy said, "Bingley here is also engaged to Miss Kitty's and Miss Elizabeth's elder sister, Miss Jane Bennet."

Lady Catherine turned to Bingley.

"Is this true, sir?" she asked Bingley.

"It is indeed, madam," Bingley said, sitting up straighter in his seat. "We are very much in love and I long to marry her when the nearest opportunity arises."

"What has prevented you?"

"She is a governess to a wealthy family in Milton, the Kirkpatricks. She promised that she wouldn't marry me until she found an adequate replacement for herself."

"Well, then you must not marry in Milton. You should tell your fiancée that she ought to marry with her sister, Kitty, here at Rosings Park's parsonage. It really makes all the sense in the world. I will organize everything. Bingley, I know what is best. Nothing could be more delightful than a double wedding."

Bingley, happy to always be obliging, agreed to this. After all, he saw the sense in it, and nothing could be more natural than for a double wedding.

"Well, that is all settled and will bring joy to the county. I will write to all the most important families in Kent, and you must stay for all the dinner parties that you will be invited to. Yes, leave everything to me. The wedding clothes and the ladies' new trousseau must all be organized. I know best and I know what to order."

"Then," Darcy finalized, "if you find it amenable to hold

a double wedding, then perhaps you might undertake the concept of a triple wedding."

Lady Catherine's brow furrowed at this. Not out of alarm, but rather out of intense curiosity.

"Triple wedding? There's another attachment in the family?"

"Yes, it is."

"Who is getting married?"

"Aunt, I am."

She squinted.

"What?"

"I am engaged to be married. To Miss Elizabeth Bennet."

When hearing this, Lady Catherine's eyes widened.

"You are engaged to be married to her?"

Darcy sighed. He had hoped that after hearing so much news that would occupy her time as well as newly found happiness, his announcement would not cause her any sort of distress. But it might not be so. For, despite that Anne had passed away, despite that nothing could be helped, and despite that both cousins never wanted to marry in the first place, Lady Catherine still viewed him as the man who she intended her daughter to marry.

"Yes, Aunt," Darcy responded, "I am engaged to Miss Elizabeth Bennet, and I ask for your blessing."

"Then...you were attached to her the entire time that Anne was ill. Darcy, I am ashamed of you. That is the coldest thing that I have ever heard, and I am disgraced by you."

"Aunt," Darcy responded, incredulous, "when did I ever learn that Anne was ill? You never sent me a word nor sentence of the matter, and I only learned of her illness after she passed away. You never told me anything. How can my actions be rendered heartless when I was ignorant of the matter?"

"Either way, it is outrageous and monstrous. You were making love to a woman while you were intended for another."

"But I told you that Anne never wanted me, nor welcomed any attachment in that direction. She is gone, Aunt. Why, when she is free from all earthly woes, do you persist in dragging her into an alliance that she never wanted?"

Lady Catherine huffed, and looked away, stubborn as ever.

"Her woes are over, and her soul is free to fly anywhere," Darcy finalized, "so let it be. For her sake."

Suddenly, Darcy came upon another tactic. Never before had he resorted his mentality to this level of scheming and manipulation. But the sooner that he could be wed to Elizabeth, the better. Besides, he was, in all essentials, still telling the truth.

"And it hurts me, aunt," Darcy added, "that you welcome Colonel Fitzwilliam's intended nuptials, as well as Bingley's, but not mine. You have joyfully planned on what to do for their wedding, intending a double wedding, but you have not welcomed mine. I propose a triple wedding, done under your care and planning, and you cast me down. Why? Why am I not allowed the same happiness that you give to Bingley's wedding plans, when I am your nephew? Would you not assist me in planning my happy day?"

And that had done the trick! For vanity, sweet vanity, will always be the weakest spot to any human who had a void within them that needed to be filled. When hearing that she would be able to organize everything, that she, Lady Catherine de Bourgh, would plan a triple wedding at Rosings Park, her mind changed over once again. It would be a wedding that would be the talk of the county for months. They would be invited to parties from all the prominent families in Kent. They would make such a marvelous debut in London. And even more, two cousins and a friend of the family would be marrying three sisters descended from landed gentry. Rosings Park would be alive with such news and would look stronger than ever. It would have an heir, and with any luck, Lady Catherine would be able to declare that she had brought it all about.

Her daughter was gone, and now she would need company more than ever. Colonel Fitzwilliam's marriage would oblige him to remain often at Rosings Park, and he would also bring a naïve bride with him, who Lady Catherine would have to shape into being the future mistress of the place. But since Colonel Fitzwilliam and Darcy were dear friends, Darcy, Bingley, Georgiana, and the others would desire to visit. Her family would be closer to her than ever. Despite losing Anne, Lady Catherine was still good at calculation, and the advantages was entirely on her side.

"Then let it be rightly understood," Lady Catherine said, "everything shall be left to me. The arrangements, engagement parties, and invitations to all the respectable homes in the county. Make it known to your future brides that I expect to arrange them to be presented at court as well. Those are my terms."

"But surely," Darcy said, "at least our ladies can choose their gowns?"

"Yes," Bingley said, "can they at least confer on that score?"

"I must approve of their gown. That is the final word on the matter."

Darcy and Bingley looked at each other. Their thoughts were the same: they were agreeing too much without consulting their fiancées. This could either go very well, or very badly. But there was nothing for it.

"Very well," Darcy said, "that can be done. Aunt, you have made me a happy man this day. Our fiancées have lost their mother. It would be nice to have a lady to oversee them during our special time."

"They should come to Rosings Park immediately," Lady Catherine said. "Since they are to be my new nieces, they should come immediately for not only the arrangements, but also to pay respects to dear Anne."

"When we return to Milton, we shall write to you as soon as we can of when we will bring our ladies back down South. Sadly, there are so many complications in Milton, that we cannot bring them down as soon as we would wish."

"But, with any luck," Mr. Bingley added, "we shall present them at Rosings within a month's time. However, nothing is fully fixed."

"You had better tell these ladies to get a move-on," Lady Catherine urged. "In fact, give them a time limit on these complications. Tell them that I shall expect them here within a month's time. That will be sufficient enough time for me to mourn my poor daughter and be ready for them. That is my final word."

Darcy knew it was better not to argue, therefore, he gave in to her demand.

While Lady Catherine did miss her daughter with every waking moment, she was a woman who could multitask mentally.

As she was regretting the loss of Anne, she had already

set her mind to ordering the spineless reverend on how she wanted the church to be decorated, how the gowns would look, who would be invited, and the invitation to St. James's Court that would soon follow. Lady Catherine would have someone to reign over, and some of those were people whom she loved. She didn't care much at all for the Bennet sisters, but since they were a means to an end for her continual happiness, their presence in her life would do very nicely.

When Bingley and Darcy once more got a word between themselves, Darcy was uneasy.

"I just made a decision without consulting Elizabeth. She is going to kill me."

"Yes, she just might." Bingley chuckled.

"Oh, shift, will you!"

The next day, both gentlemen left Rosings Park with a lighter step.

Their future was set, and a certain cousin and his bride was saved from a difficult life. Such success!

For what must be done cannot be done too quickly at all.

Chapter 10

Proper Protocol

The next day was delightful, for it was one of my days off. Charlotte was able to stay with me that day, and Margaret had come to visit us.

Maria, on the other hand, had gone with Jane to meet the Kirkpatrick family and apply as a candidate for Jane's replacement. For all her slight apprehensions on the matter, Maria was still interested in securing the post.

Kitty and Rasby also were given the day off, and they were going on an outing with Colonel Fitzwilliam and Mr. Bell.

When Margaret arrived, she was a little agitated.

"I went to visit Nicholas and Mary Higgins before I came," Margaret said.

"Nicholas isn't working?" I asked.

"He still is not working."

"He hasn't gone back to applying at Hampers?"

"Even if he wanted to, which he doesn't, would they hire him again? Think, he is known for leading the strike, and because of Boucher, he is guilty by association."

"But they have no income coming in."

"That is why I asked Mary if she was willing to work for us. Dixon has often been wishing to find a servant to help her in the household duties. Mary Higgins has agreed to it, and that will help them maintain themselves."

I rubbed her shoulder, grateful.

"Happy thought. Well done." I looked at her and still saw food in her basket.

"Food for Mrs. Boucher and their children?"

"Yes."

"Kitty brought them food yesterday. Boucher still has not come home."

"He's still in hiding. And no one will talk to him."

Charlotte entered, putting on her coat.

"Who will not talk to who?" she asked, overhearing the last sentence.

Once we informed Charlotte of where we were going, she was fascinated. Charlotte was aware of the riot because I had written to her about it. However, I never recollected telling her about Boucher's wife, therefore, when we escorted Margaret to the Boucher residence, I had to fill her in on the details.

"So," Charlotte concluded, "even Mrs. Boucher doesn't know where her husband is?"

"Even if she does," I deduced, "why would she tell us? If I were her, I wouldn't."

"I don't think she does know," Margaret said, "because she has a tendency to speak very meanly of him. I don't think she would do that if he told her where he was."

"This Boucher," Charlotte continued, "the man who started the riot, has gone into hiding even from his own family. I can see why she is angry with him. Especially since you told me that he has six children, Lizzy."

We arrived at the Boucher residence, and Mrs. Boucher saw us immediately. Ushering us inside, Margaret laid out the food she had, and Mrs. Boucher began to separate it immediately, putting it on different plates to distribute among the children.

"A fine mess their dad has put us through," Mrs. Boucher said as she laid out the food and all the children began to eat veraciously.

When seeing the squalor and living conditions that the Bouchers underwent, I could tell that Charlotte was disturbed. Before her very eyes were the very gray that clouded over Milton and threatened any vibrancy that could exist in the place. There was poor in Hertfordshire. There were definite lower classes, and every now and again, gypsies did wander through the Hertfordshire woodlands. However, this was her first real encounter with true destitution. Therefore, the reality of her new potential residence was made even more apparent, and I wondered if it shook her resolve further.

"Perhaps Boucher stays away from home for your own good," Margaret offered, "as a means of keeping you safe."

"Of course, tha's what he done did," Mrs. Boucher retorted, eating some of the food herself, "but we wouldn' be in this righ' mess if he hadn't caused that riot at Marlborough Mills to begin with. And if only there had neve' been a strike to begin with. I'd curse all those committee men myself, even Nicholas, but Nicholas has been kind to me, so he's the only one I forgive. But gettin' it into their minds tha' another strike was a good idea. And now look where we are. We're worse off than ever."

Mrs. Boucher suddenly became more aware of Charlotte, who stood behind us as we listened to her grievances.

"Goodness me," Mrs. Boucher said, "and we don' know each other a bit, now do we?"

"Oh, this is my friend from the South," I said, "Miss Charlotte Lucas."

"Well," Mrs. Boucher said, "Miss Lucas, forgive me for not givin' yer friends' the time to make yer acquaintance. I was jus' so happy to have food for my littleuns."

"No offense was taken, I assure you," Charlotte Lucas responded. "What are you children's names?"

"That one there is John," Mrs. Boucher answered, gesturing to each child, "the other is Mina, then there's Joshua, Jonathan, Hester, and this littleun here is Jacob." With the last one, she gestured to the baby that she was cradling in her arms. "Their father's name is John, so we settled on all the boys' names startin' with 'J'."

"An interesting idea. It makes sense, in many ways."

Mrs. Boucher turned to Margaret and me.

"Thank ee' for the food again. If Boucher doesn't come back, I don' want to make yer a crutch for me to be always leanin' on."

"I'm certain," Margaret replied, "that once all the devastation is over and the strike becomes nothing more than a memory, Boucher will find work again."

"I'm not certain of tha'," Mrs. Boucher replied, sullen and solemn, "when it comes to my husband, I'm sure of nothin'. If yer were married to such a man, yer wouldn't be either." Suddenly, she realized how depressing she was being, and she rose out of it. "Sorry, yer didn' come here for no sad tales. Or about how I regret all of my life."

This last sentence was so painful that none of us knew how to respond from that.

Soon, we made our excuses and left.

"I am happy that we didn't linger," Charlotte said, "but I hope she didn't think it was rude of us."

"She didn't," I assured her, "the problem when someone does a good deed for you is that they remain in your life for too long. When someone is often helping you, sometimes, you just want the help, but don't want their lingering company. In fact, I wouldn't be surprised if she wished she could receive our help and never have to see us that much."

"It makes sense. After all, who wants to constantly be in the presence of someone that they owe much to? It's a strange sort of situation."

"Well," I said, "now that charity has been dispensed with, it would be best if we get you acquainted with some more people in Milton. Besides, I really ought to speak with Darcy's friend. You will at least be interested in this next venture, Charlotte. We'll take you to Marlborough Mills."

Margaret Hale stopped dead in her tracks.

"What?"

Ah yes, I should have been more prepared for this. Oh well, there was nothing for it.

"Margaret, before Darcy left, he wanted to make certain that Thornton knew I was safe. It seems proper that I inform Thornton about Charlotte's arrival. Darcy would not want me to be estranged from his friend."

Margaret showed no emotion, for it was her habit.

"Very well."

"If you had other arrangements, I would understand. But I would like it if you joined us."

"No, I have no prior engagements at all. If you wish for my company, then yes, I would be happy to oblige you."

"Thank you," I replied, grateful to her. For, whatever be the situation between her and Thornton, it would feel awkward to visit Marlborough Mills without her. I would feel as if I was missing a half to an equation that I was part of.

When we walked to Marlborough Mills, it gave Charlotte the chance to see more of Milton. Since it was a whole new experience for her, every new street offered a sort of wonderment, even when it was not an aesthetically pleasing sight. Novelty was, after all, novelty.

As such, when we reached a particularly busy street, Charlotte couldn't help but be inattentive to us and just stand there, marveling at everything while we waited for some carriages to go by.

This distraction was precisely what Margaret had wanted, and perhaps so did I. It would give me the chance to explain myself, and for Margaret to satisfy her curiosity. After all, I did owe her an explanation.

"Why did you invite me along for going to see Thornton? I was not needed."

"I won't even deny that a part of it is selfish reasons. It would be strange going to Marlborough Mills without you. I can't tell you why, for it is not a logical sentiment, but it is what it is. Besides, this will be good for you anyway."

"And how so, pray?"

"Because you need to make peace with Thornton."

Margaret sighed.

"Why do you always do this to me? I can only feel as I feel. And you have to understand...what happened with you and Darcy will not happen with Thornton and me. We are different than you both."

"Yes, you are. But this is something else."

"What, then?"

"I need you to learn something that I have taken the time to learn: that easily there can be friendship after heartache. After disappointed affections. Just like there can be strong friendship after flaws are acknowledged. You and Thornton can be friends. And right now, you need those."

"I need little in life. I know how to survive."

"Yes but let us be honest. Bessy is gone. Soon, all of us Bennets will be gone back down South. And your mother is not well. Margaret, right now, it would do well to have friends. I don't want you alone."

Margaret looked at Charlotte, who a little girl came up to and asked for a penny. Charlotte was reaching into her purse to give her one.

"Charlotte and Maria are here," Margaret declared, "and Rasby might still be here as well."

"We don't know that yet. We don't know if they will replace us...and when Kitty leaves, we don't know what Rasby will do. And Plato moves around with his regiment. Margaret, I do not want to leave you here, like this."

No matter her prejudices on the matter, Margaret was still logical. She could see the sense behind my worries.

"Very well. But I will only do it for the sake that being kind is a very moral thing to do, and not for my own interests."

"Good. Your selfless reasons balance out my selfish ones. I can work with that."

Margaret chuckled.

"We really are different."

"Don't worry," I laughed, "we're not as different as you think. And even if we were, I don't think it would matter very much."

Charlotte came back to us, her cheeks a little red from being interested in her surroundings.

"Sorry. I was busy looking at everything. Did I make you wait?"

"Not at all," I assured her. "I'm just happy that you are curious. Now, we march onward!" I said, like a military general. "The sooner we get there, the sooner you will see a sight that really will be all new to you."

We walked onward and soon we arrived at Marlborough Mills.

When we arrived, Charlotte's eyes widened even more. Due to her limited exposure with factories in London, she had never stepped foot in a manufacturing company before. Therefore, to see all the hustle and bustle of it all was a little fascinating. Even from the exterior, there was enough of the machinery to see, and she needed a moment.

"This is Marlborough Mills?" Charlotte asked.

"Yes, it is," I said, "It's owned by John Thornton. He's a manufacturer and magistrate. He's Mr. Darcy's friend."

Lowering her voice, Charlotte leaned into us.

"Is this where the riot took place?" she asked.

"Yes, it is."

"And Mr. Boucher was the man who led it."

"He never intended any violence," Margaret assured her, "but it happened all the same."

"I just...well, it makes sense to not be afraid of a place where you were once a victim in. After all, no building or business is guilty of the actions of the humans within them. Yet, I still wonder that you can come with such fortitude. Then again, you both are stronger than I."

We began to walk to the factory, to have a word with Mr. Thornton, when Margaret and I passed some older acquaintances of ours.

"Liam, Colin, Robert, and John!" I cried.

Up ahead, heading out of the sorting room, were the four Irishmen that had fought with us against the mob that had overtaken the factory.

Eagerly Margaret and I dashed up to them, happy to see that they were still healthy and hearty.

"Miss Bennet and Miss Hale," Colin said as they all removed their hats, out of respect, "you come to visit."

"A short visit, but a visit nevertheless," Margaret said, merrily, "how have you four been?"

"Alive," John responded, "this land hasn't killed us yet."

"And for some of us, we only have to survive it for one more week," Robert added.

"What does that mean?" Then I remembered Charlotte behind me. "Oh, pray, forgive me. I forgot to introduce my friend, Charlotte Lucas. Charlotte, this is Liam, Robert, Colin, and John. They are all from Wexford, Ireland."

"It's a pleasure to make your acquaintance," Charlotte said, offering her hand to shake. Margaret and I each gave a knowing look; Charlotte was adapting very well.

Like us, Charlotte smiled happily and met the Irishmen with a pleasant demeanor. Men are like us women: they require a favorable opinion and often respond in kind. When seeing Margaret and I, the men already were softened, because they knew we found their company pleasant. But now, with another woman from the South, who had decided to meet them with no hostility of the kind, it livened them even more.

After common pleasantries were exchanged, I couldn't

help but return back to the subject that they had mentioned before.

"What do you mean that you will not have to suffer for more than a week? Does that indicate that you are leaving Milton?"

"Many of us have thought on the idea and thought it was best," Robert added.

"Does that mean that you are leaving, Robert?"

He blushed.

"It's best that he does," Liam answered for him. "He's got family back in Wexford and Belfast. There's more for him there."

"Answering for me, are you?" Robert retaliated. "When did I give you permission to do that?"

"When you were blushing so hard that you couldn't even respond to her."

"Shut it!" Robert replied, shoving Liam's shoulder.

"How many of the Irish are going back home?" Charlotte asked, hoping to show an interest.

"Over half of us," John responded. "You must understand, most of the women were shaken up after the violence here. And some of the men aren't at the age where they can defend themselves or are able to learn a new trade. Pliable education is for the young. But as for the violence, it's not their fault. Sometimes, there is nothing wrong with running away. In fact, sometimes it can lead to your survival."

"And what of you three?" Margaret pursued, "are you three going back as well?"

"I am," Liam answered, "but let it be rightly understood. I'm not leaving out of fear."

"Then why are you going back?"

"I came here to do something new and to see new things. I came here to see what more life had in store for me. Then I saw it. And the world saw me. It scared me and it hurt me. I saw life. And it made me realize that perhaps nothing can compare to home sometimes. I fought, I survived, now I have the right to find peace where I may. You see, Miss Bennet, Miss Hale, and Miss Lucas, sometimes we realize that we have the right to rest and be easy. Even if nothing is certain."

I turned to Colin and John.

"And what about you both?"

"Oh, we're staying," Colin responded. "That's plain and flat."

"And what makes you do that?" Margaret asked. "I understand why Liam and Robert want to return home, but why stay here with us? I do not wish to sound impertinent, but I am starved to understand why you want to be here, after all that has happened."

"For me," John answered, "I've got no one back home. No farm, no house, no certain post. When the unknown faces you from behind, all you have is the world ahead. Even the worst bits of it."

"For me, it's something else," Colin spoke. "Something darker."

"Darker?" I repeated.

"Yes. Ladies, when something happens to you, when there is violence against you just because of what you were born as, an anger rises up. Your instinct may be to run, but it quickly gets devoured by a bitterness. A wrath. I want to stay and have everyone see my face. And remember what they do to us. It makes you want to stand up and say, 'No more. I won't let you do this again.' The only way that I can do that is if I stay. And I make them remember me."

"I'd like to say that we'll overcome this one day," I admitted, "but I really don't know, Colin. All I can tell you is good luck. And don't die anytime soon."

"I won't," Colin said, grinning. "I'm ugly as sin, but I've got a lucky face."

The four men's attention was seized by looking past us and to their left. We followed their gaze and saw Mr. Thornton watching us from the steps of the factory.

When seeing us, his gaze was as steely as ever. Really, between him and Mr. Darcy, I wondered what sort of talent that they both possessed between the two of them.

"Well," Robert said, buckling under his employer's gaze, "we had best be getting on with our work."

"Unless we are fortunate," Margaret said to Robert and Liam, "we might never see each other again."

"No, we might not," Liam responded, his gaze the firmest, "and that is the woe of it, I suppose."

Instead of shaking our hands, they bowed to us.

We curtsied in return.

"Acting like men of the South, are you?" I asked, with my eyes twinkling.

"No, I gather. Rather, like proper Irishmen. Thank you, ladies of England, for thinking us worthy of being loved."

Startled by his earnest response, I blushed.

"Be safe, wherever you go. We will always want you to be happy."

"If only we could guarantee that," Robert finalized, then they all went inside the factory as Mr. Thornton approached us.

As Thornton drew closer, he removed his hat. Beside me, I felt Margaret's blush, even though she did not display it.

"Brave heart, Margaret," I whispered to her.

"Lizzy," Margaret responded, equally low, "you know

very well that my courage rises with every attempt to intimidate me."

"Yes, I do know that."

Thornton reached us at last.

"Miss Bennet and Miss Hale," Mr. Thornton responded, "you come to visit the Mill."

"We do indeed, sir," I said for the rest of us. "My fiancé informed me that I should speak with you, from time to time, to assure you that I am well. In this respect, I prefer to oblige him."

"And you left me remiss in my duties. After work, I was planning on calling on you at your home, to inquire after your well-being."

"I beat you to the deed."

"Yes," he found himself unable to suppress a smile, "you did indeed."

"Also, I have another duty. Two ladies and good friends of mine have visited from Hertfordshire. One of them is present. Mr. Thornton, this is my dear friend, Miss Charlotte Lucas, of Lucas Lodge. Charlotte, this is Mr. Thornton, of Marlborough Mills."

They both made introductions.

"Might I praise the look of your factory, sir," Charlotte asked. "Or would a compliment be disarming? I confess that I am ignorant of industry, therefore, my praises must be miniscule."

"If you speak out of intelligence or ignorance, I shall take the compliment keenly. Thank you, Miss Lucas."

"My friends will not remain in Milton for long," I continued, "therefore, I was wondering if your mother and sister might be willing to allowing us to visit them one day this week?"

"If you are willing to submit to a little bit of spontaneity,"

Thornton responded, "then I can send word to my mother, and she can tell the cook that you three will remain for dinner."

"Oh, we should not," Margaret said at last. Her suddenness of speaking had forced Thornton to look at her. Feeling heat rise up within her, Margaret felt the need to explain her meaning. "I do not mean to offend, but I worry that your mother will not enjoy us inviting ourselves to a dinner on the day of visiting. I am aware that you might know your mother more than I, but I do not wish to put Charlotte in the way of making a bad first impression."

"My mother will understand that I have made the request. Your concern for my mother's comfort is well-meaning, but by staying, you help me in honoring Darcy's request to see to Miss Bennet's comfort. Miss Hale, you must understand my desire to consider my friends, mustn't you?"

Margaret did not reply, because her spirit could not possibly have done so. When speaking with her, Thornton had returned her appeals with a firm gaze that had a deep intent within them. It was as if his eyes were saying, 'you hurt me, but I will not turn away. I will look upon you. You will see me for what I am'.

The eyes of a proud man who had been rejected.

It was a look that I had seen before.

It was a look that I had known before.

And had experienced before.

Whether she liked it or not, Margaret could neither ignore it nor turn away from it.

All she could do was return his look with a fearless one of her own. She had her courage and heaven forbid anyone take it away from her.

"If our company will neither distress nor vex Mrs.

Thornton," Margaret responded, "then could a note be sent to Crampton, informing my parents of where I am?"

Thornton looked at her, determined in his resolution, but his eyes twinkled with a sense of victory.

"That will be done."

———

"In the meantime," Thornton said, "allow me to show Miss Lucas around Marlborough Mills. Miss Lucas, if you would do me the honor, you could become acquainted with factory life. Milton thrives through industry, and it is industry that maintains England."

"And since I am all in support of the thriving of English civilization," Charlotte responded, "I am interested." Charlotte turned to us. "Can we tour the place? I am, after all, curious."

"Yes, you may. I was just about to make my rounds about the place. Giving you a tour would only give me company."

Thornton led the way, and we all crowded around him as we entered the carding room and the rest of the factory. Overcome by the amount of cotton in the air and the smell, Charlotte had to cover her mouth with a handkerchief, but from the workers to the visual spectacle that was before our very eyes, Charlotte was attentive. Whenever Thornton explained what each room did and the steps to cotton being made, it was interesting, to say the least.

Around twenty minutes into the tour, the overseer returned to tell us that Mrs. Thornton was able to inform her cook and that we would dine with them. Also, now being aware that we had a visitor, she was willing to receive her within a half an hour.

This was well, until I recalled that we would be dining

with Fanny Thornton. The mind will always reel at the foolish steps that we allow ourselves to take. In my desire to connect with Thornton and augment Margaret's allies in Milton, I had quite forgotten of the broken heart that was Fanny Thornton. What was even worse was that she was perhaps suffering under the weight of disappointed affections from a man who might have been her first large love. Darcy had never done anything to show any particular regard for her, but when did that ever stop a person from feeling for someone? Also, Darcy, despite his traditional stoic demeanor, was awe-inspiring and had a way of fascinating a ladies' emotions. Caroline Bingley was proof of that.

And come to think of it... one day I would have to see Caroline Bingley again!

The terror of so many uncomfortable acquaintances would not shake me, but it did vex me. After all, no one looks forward to an uncomfortable encounter.

Having twenty more minutes before we had to go to the house and introduce Charlotte to Mrs. Thornton and Fanny, it gave us more time with Thornton.

At some point, Charlotte had neared me as she watched the children gathering the remaining cotton from the floor, under the workers.

"They have to be eight or nine years old," Charlotte whispered to me.

"Yes, they do. Too young. Then again, everyone is always too young, or too innocent, and they have to suffer the worst of it."

"I feel so very spoiled."

"No, I will not have that," I objected. "Some of us have been born fortunate, and others weren't. That is not our fault. Besides, I do not regret my life, nor do I regret one happy moment. Nor should you. All we can do is see if we can assist those where we may."

With a quizzical eye, she looked at me squarely.

"You have become more sensible than me, haven't you?"

"I have been more out in the world. When you do, you will not learn to feel ashamed because of our better life. Rather, it will be the reverse. You will cling to the happier moments more and it will be the foil on which you set off all the other moments. Don't cling to shame, Charlotte. The world rules us with that too much already."

Charlotte continued to watch the workers when I noticed that Thornton had casually walked up next to Margaret and began talking to her. I wondered what they were speaking about...

Chapter 11

A Strained Romance

When he had seen the Southern ladies first enter Marlborough Mills from his window, Thornton had found himself compelled, against all logic, to go down and see them.

His plan to visit Elizabeth Bennet had been anticipated by their coming, and she had brought a stranger with her... along with the woman who had rejected his marriage proposal.

By rights, he should have no desire to speak to Margaret Hale. In fact, logic seemed to be entirely against him. And yet, he loved her more than ever. The irony of this all was not something he dwelled on, but rather, he had to accept.

Yet, as he had rushed from his office to meet them, he was aware all would end with him cursing his weak nature. Margaret's company would give him none of the satisfaction that he craved for. In fact, it would leave him starved. But there was nothing for it.

Besides, he had to do right by Darcy anyway. So, his inability to control his romantic inclinations was made up for by attending to Elizabeth.

When he had actively walked toward the ladies, he found that they were not alone, but talking with the Irishmen that had stood by them when the mob descended on Marlborough Mills. At first, Thornton halted, watching them from the shadows of a cart that he stood behind. He had heard every other third or fourth word that was spoken and learned that Colin and John were remaining behind. He knew of the number of Irish that were to remain, but did not recall all their names. While he had watched, he saw how Margaret still displayed a sympathy for the workers who defended Elizabeth... in a manner that she would never show to him. His heart was wounded at the prospect that she would never display any sort of sympathy toward himself, or anything like affection. Sadly, his heart was awake, and there was no chance of it falling asleep again. He was lost in the oblivion that was her rejection. And there he would have to remain until time lessened the burden.

Finally, he felt that he had the right to intercede, which he did when the moment presented itself.

When seeing him, Liam, Robert, Colin, and John dispersed—truly, it made Thornton feel like he had the plague! Next, he had approached the ladies, made Charlotte Lucas's acquaintance, and had begun showing her around the factory.

Then, as fate would have it, Charlotte had found her way by Lizzy's side, giving him the chance to walk alongside Margaret Hale. Immediately having done so, his tongue froze. He had no notion of what to say.

Now was the moment...what should he do?

At first, Thornton was silent and so was Margaret. Neither one of them knew how to begin, or even if they wanted to.

Margaret felt the strain of awkwardness that always presented themselves to them both, but she was quite tired of it. She neither wanted to be uncomfortable nor anxious. Therefore, there was nothing for it, but for her to confront the matter.

"I know that my presence is hard for you," she began, "so I thank you for seeing us willingly, and for offering us to dine with your mother. I am sure that she does not wish to see me at all."

"She will do her best to be tolerant in your presence," Thornton responded, willing to be equally frank, "but in truth, you are correct. Your company is not one that she would prefer. Do not take offense, but no mother would ever prefer to be in the company of a woman who rejected her son."

"Yes, I can understand that her resentment is natural. But you and I know the truth; she never preferred my company to begin with."

"As to that, I never understood why."

Margaret looked at him, surprised.

"You didn't?"

"Well, not initially. Over time, I realized that her dislike might have been founded on some misunderstandings between you both, but quickly it occurred to me that she was prejudiced from the very beginning. She seemed to be wholly against me meeting a lady from the South."

"Did she?"

"Yes, I believe she did. I do not say these things to harm you, Miss Hale. But we have always had a way of being painfully honest with each other."

"I am not upset over it. In fact, I am happy to be enlightened on the matter."

"Are you?" Thornton asked, raising an eyebrow.

"Yes, I am. It would explain many things, including her natural discomfort around me. What prompted the initial dislike? Was it a contempt for Southern people in general, or was there something about me, in particular?"

"It began as a general sort of dislike. You must understand that my mother comes from a place of pride in the industry that we cultivate here. The South has always been a life that my mother does not accept. It's a lazy sort of existence, in her eyes, filled with people who are idle and ladies who wish to marry the richest man that they can find. Has this subject offended you?"

"I will not deny that it has. You must understand, Mr. Thornton, that it is not a delight to be despised just for being as one is and born as what one is born as."

"I can very well understand the feeling; for is that not how you initially regarded me and kind such as myself? Do you know what it felt like to hear you say that you do not want to understand me?"

Margaret blinked, a little unnerved by the notion that she had taken a step too far somewhere. Surely, he was being too cruel in his assessment against her. However, there was one aspect of her character that could never be ignored: her logical side.

"Yes," Margaret responded, "I did say that. Perhaps I was wrong to."

"You really think this of me? You really don't want to try and understand the sort of creature that I am?"

"I spoke too hastily, and from the place of a woman who was offered another proposal that she was neither prepared for, nor wanted."

When hearing this, Thornton felt as if a sliver of ice had been slashed through his heart.

She knew not how she had tortured him, and the pain of it all was so very overwhelming to bear. However, one does as one does, and Thornton's expression barely shifted. Only his eyes betrayed him. But that was enough. When looking at him, Margaret saw the heartbreak in his eyes. Knowing that she was the cause of it did not lead to her becoming colder, but she was stricken with a sudden desire to ease his pain. She ought to care, even if she did not love.

"You were a gentleman," she said, "to propose in the way that you did."

What did she call him? This sudden remark, a remark which Thornton knew was something that Margaret praised highly, was enough to open his wonder, swell his pride, and give him a sense of hope—vain hope, that perhaps she did not despise him as he believed.

"You said that I was not."

"When a woman receives an offer of marriage that she did not anticipate," Margaret explained, "the wrong things can be said. Even if I do not regret how I feel now, nor do I regret how I felt then, I do... I am wondering now that I did not respond properly myself. I could have been kinder to you, but I did not know how to at the time. I just... I do not want to marry anyone at the moment, nor do I feel the impulse to. Whatever hardships that I have experienced in Milton, I still—well, all I know is my own sense of autonomy, my own freedom. Oh, I am explaining it all incorrectly, I gather."

"No, I can understand that."

Looking at him more directly, Margaret wondered if he was telling her the truth, or if he was saying that for the sake of connecting to her. But the joy of it all was that Thornton always had a habit of telling the absolute truth, no matter who he spoke with.

"Can you?"

"Miss Hale, what do you think I have been fighting to do since my father died? I worked hard to be free of the debts that he left. I worked harder to have the house that would free my mother and sister of hardship. I worked harder to become a master and rule my own life. Don't you see? Freedom is the most God-given right that we all deserve, but it seems to be the hardest thing for us to have and keep hold of. We both want freedom, in our own way. Right now, you want freedom of your own. Why didn't you just tell me this? I would have understood."

"Like I said, I was dazed and distraught from the sudden proposal—a proposal that I did not expect. I was confused, and now I see that I did not say the right things myself. I don't want to hurt you, Mr. Thornton. Even when we disagreed with each other, it was never designed to hurt you. I just speak as I do, for the sake of freedom that you understand so well. What am I if not my right to be free in thought and question where I will? I would be in agony if I was not allowed to be otherwise. That was why I left London when I did."

"What do you mean that you left London?"

"I was raised in London. I was my cousin's companion, so I spent years there. Well, I realized that I would never be happy there, for I wanted to be a part of the common folk's lives, which is what my father did in Hampshire. I wanted to no longer be a part of the pretense of the circles that I revolved in, of the veneer of that sort of lifestyle. I wanted truth, I suppose, simple truth, where I didn't have to feel like I was drawn down by a false and flimsy existence. I wanted to feel a part of everything, while also exploring the freedoms that didn't come from always having to take a carriage every-where and being confined by drawing rooms. That was what was waiting for me back in the London circles. I didn't know if I could bear to continue on that way after Edith left. Edith was the cousin who I was the companion to."

"Do you miss her?"

"For a time, I did miss her. But when Elizabeth joined me and then we found Kitty, Jane, and Lydia here, there was nothing wanting very much. And then there was Bessy..."

"I am sorry for that."

"I know that you are. And I know that, considering your position, there may have been very little you could do about that. After all, it was the workers who cannot make up their mind if they want a wheel in the factories or not. And I also have to accept that Bessy told me herself that she wanted to go into the Carding Room, where she fell ill. It's just... between how we first met, and what happened to Bessy, it's hard for me to forget these things."

"Maybe the problem is that we never took the time to talk of subjects that were vital to helping one understand each other. Maybe this never gave us time to also confront the differences in one another and find a way for it to always end in a peaceful way as opposed to discord."

"That is quite true. We really don't know each other very well, do we?"

"No, I suppose we don't. Now that I think on the matter, I suppose it was foolish of me, wasn't it?"

"What was?"

"To propose to you the way that I did. You are right; we don't know each other. Therefore, how can you marry someone when you still do not know all the aspects of their character?"

"There is one woman who believes that it is better to

know as little about the other person's character before you marry them," Margaret quipped, chuckling a little. "But I find that I could never submit to such an edict."

"What woman is that?" Thornton asked.

Margaret looked at Charlotte, and her expression said it all, without her wishing to. Thornton followed her gaze and watched Charlotte as she spoke with Elizabeth.

"It is not my words to have repeated," Margaret said, "perhaps I was being impertinent. I don't want you thinking ill of anyone, especially a worthy creature."

"I won't," Thornton assured her. "If a person does want to catch a husband or wife, I suppose that it is a wise prescription."

"It is, and we all have the right to choose our lives. Besides, she would never marry without reason."

"I'm sure that she would not."

"Thank you."

Margaret looked at him.

"Do you know something strange? It is nonsensical if you are not afraid to learn of it."

"What is that?"

"I have never been frightened of you, but there has always been an awkwardness, hasn't there been? I am not afraid to talk of this matter, because it is best to confront it. But I am not uncomfortable now. I cannot explain it. I am not uncomfortable now."

Thornton did not face her, but his stern brow did diminish slightly, as he stared ahead and processed all that she had said.

"Is that what you feel now?" He asked.

"Yes. And what of you? Do you feel better at all, or less so?"

"I don't know what I feel."

"That is a natural reaction as well, I suppose. Maybe I am bringing you into a state of confusion."

"I love you."

The woes and anxieties all surfaced in Margaret's mind once more. Mingling the pressures of such a statement with the contrariness of the situation, compiled with the disappointment that arises from returning discord, Margaret was at a loss of what to say. At first. Yet the fact remained that a response was expected, a reaction was owed, and Thornton needed her firmness if he was to ever move on from the matter.

"Thornton," Margaret began, sighing, "why? Why must you return to such an unpleasant subject for us?"

"Because it ought to be said, but not as a reason to draw you in, make you uncomfortable, or have you retract your statement of calling me a gentleman. No, it is not that at all. I do not say it out of a desire to get you to feel as I do."

"Then why say it?"

"I need you to know what's in my heart, so that you are more prepared for the awkwardness that can arise from time to time. That you know why I look on you sometimes. Why I am aware of where you are, whenever you are in the same room as myself. Why I listen to every word you say, even when it is not directed toward myself. But whatever are my feelings, I don't want them to frighten you. Nor be unnerved by them. I told you that I love now, and I will love, regardless of it being returned or not. I expect nothing anymore. I am aware that *that* door is closed to me, perhaps forever. But what I wish for you to know is that you need never shy away from me, because of it. I can only imagine how frightening my feelings for you are, in your eyes. Am I correct?"

"Yes," Margaret answered simply, "I admit to being terrified by inspiring such feeling from someone."

"Yes, I suspect as such. I can assure you, Miss Hale, that my feelings are harmless. When you see me, I would like for you to look on me as a friend. My feelings do not have to separate us. Do we not have the right to try and have a warmer regard for the other? I do not want us to always be making each other angry either."

"And you promise me that you will do this, with no expectations, no pressure against me, and no sense of obligation on my part. I can overlook how you feel and be your friend—I think I would like that. As long as you promise that any camaraderie between us is not an indication that I am expected to become your possession. Or anyone's for that matter."

"I promise."

The joys of the soul exhaling will always be a cathartic experience when pushed in the throes of romantic strain and back into the arms of casual acquaintances. When hearing that Thornton would be kind to them both, and not allow his passions to interrupt any potential connection between them, was a weight off her mind.

"Then I will try to be your friend," Margaret said. This newly found peace proved to be a little provocative on her basic nature. She found herself to be a little amused, and out of this amusement came a desire to be a little lighthearted and giddy. "And no kissing me again."

When hearing her lighter tone, and her somewhat joking demeanor, Thornton stole a glance at the beautiful woman that walked alongside him. Her words were censorious, but her tone was inviting. While it was natural for it to be so, especially since it was merely trying to be considerate, Thornton was starved for some form of affection from her. Thus, it led to the opposite of what Margaret had wanted or desired: it fed his optimism and offered him a sense of encouragement. It may very well have been the worst thing that one should do, however, the heart cannot help but submit to the overwhelmingly infective and oft undeniably addictive habit such as vain hope.

Thornton, like Darcy, was human. And the humanity that struck them, more deeply than it affected most around them, would swell up within them, and they found themselves riding along the waves of blind passions, the shores of uncertainty, and sailing along the winds of chance.

Chance fueled them.

It willed them onward, and they believed in it. They clung to it with a desperate need. For what are we without our dreams, no matter how unlikely they are to come true?

"Yes," he said at last, "I must not do that. But you must give me something in return."

This bargain made Margaret freeze internally. Whatever he was proposing was something that she felt unwilling to give.

"Mr. Thornton," she stated, "you have never noticed that I am not the sort of woman who prefers to bargain?"

"I know that about you all too well. But I must ask this of you anyway."

"Speak, and I shall decide what I do after this moment."

"I just request that you find some joy in seeing me. That, no matter what our past argument, each day we wake up and find something about the other's company that we like."

Now that she heard his plea, Margaret sighed internally.

"I felt that we did improve in some way, and then we regressed. I am willing to try again."

"Thank you for that. That is all that I ask. And one more thing."

"Another thing? Mr. Thornton, you are running out of favors."

He chuckled, and it forced him to genuinely smile. Having looked up at him at that precise moment, Margaret was able to see the transformation that a smile placed on him. For the first time in her life, she noticed that he was handsome. In his own unique way, his features were statuesque. It was not enough to make her feel anything, but rather, it was enough to soften her judgments.

"It is a little thing."

"How little?" she asked.

"Little, but also large. I just wish to offer my condolences again for Bessy. I can see that you miss her terribly."

———

This honest confession and heartfelt offer of regrets could not help but affect Margaret. Her breath was caught in her throat, and she felt the loss even more at that moment. All the reality of the loss had rushed back into her mind and Bessy's face came clear in her thoughts.

"You mean it," Margaret said, "you really mean it."

"Of course, I do."

Her eyes wilted and withered under his gaze.

"I know that you do. And that is the joy of it. Thank you. I do miss her. We all do. Do you know, when we went to your mother's annual dinner party, Bessy remained at our house, and she was reading a book that time. She knew how to read but never had the access to many books being at her disposal. When she saw them, her eyes widened, and she looked as if she saw a goldmine for the first time in her life.

It's not fair, Thornton. And when I say this, I am not blaming you. I am blaming the unfairness of life. She was too young. She never had a day of full happiness, from what Nicholas said."

"And I can well believe it. The life of a factory worker without savings can be an appalling existence. Especially when one doesn't understand economy. Many have died in life that deserved better. Others live for a long time, and they deserved worse. We all wish we could change the world and make the judgments of who lives and who doesn't, but what would we do with it?"

"I do not deny that, at one time of my life, I did have a desperate desire to control the world around me. But, once I accepted the humility of it all, I realized that I was not the one to judge and thank goodness for that. Better to observe, reflect, and consider things from all perspectives." Suddenly, Margaret clutched her stomach and held it.

Immediately, Thornton inquired about her.

"Are you ill? Shall I send for Doctor Donaldson?"

"No, I am quite alright, I assure you," she rushed out. "It is merely that I saw an image of Bessy when she passed away. It flashed before my eyes."

Her face changed color.

"The tragedy is affecting me again."

Instinctively, Thornton offered her his arm. Without thinking. Without any motive but to assist her.

Margaret looked at his hand and then she placed her arm in his.

"Thank you. I think, for a second, the shock returned to me. And when I think of my mother."

"Is she really very ill?"

"Yes, she is. The Doctor has told me to prepare myself. For the eventuality."

Thornton's eyes grew dark.

"Nothing is more terrifying than losing one's mother."

"Yes, it is. My Aunt Shaw raised me, but my mother was still my mother. I lost Bessy and...Thornton, I do not think I can bear to lose anymore."

"She might recover," he insisted.

"Yes, she might. I pray for it."

"But remember."

"What?"

"You have friends here."

"Thank you. Elizabeth would be proud of me right now."

"Would she?"

"Yes, I daresay that she would."

"And why is that?"

"Because I would have to tell her something that will swell her pride. I have to tell her that she might have been right."

"Oh. Telling someone that is never the easiest thing."

"No, Mr. Thornton, it is not."

―――――――

At last, it was time to go to the house and Mrs. Thornton had to assist us. Charlotte's coming had softened Mrs. Thornton somewhat, but it was very evident that she was uncomfortable around most of the women who had come to dine with them.

Margaret had to prepare herself for stiff hospitality. After all, Mrs. Thornton was obviously and evidently aware that Margaret had rejected her son. Her maternal instincts were awake, alert, and activated, and she felt the keen desire to defend her child from the coldness of a woman who did not understand her son's worth.

On Elizabeth's side, there was the problem of Fanny Thornton. It didn't matter what Elizabeth did or said. In Fanny's eyes, she was guilty of ruining all her happiness, and it could not be overcome or overridden with alacrity. No, it had to be endured, and Fanny viewed this visit of theirs as the worst crime of all.

Outwardly, she was merely quiet around Elizabeth and spoke only by way of an answer and offering polite questions. Charlotte Lucas's appearance was the largest balm of all. First, she was a new acquaintance with no prior history in Milton, therefore, Fanny could entertain her with ease. Second, Charlotte was not like Margaret, who didn't seem eager to offer much amiable conversation, for Charlotte was much less severe, and this endeared her to Fanny. Thirdly, Charlotte was physically plainer than Fanny, therefore, there was no sense of a threat. Thus, Charlotte became the most spoken to, which left her feeling a sense of self-completion. Elizabeth and Margaret would have fallen to the wayside of conversation, had it not been for Mr. Thornton.

Thornton, now feeling as if he could find an even ground with Margaret, knew how to approach discussion with her. Also, Elizabeth, who was now the fiancée of his closest friend, would naturally be easy to speak with. When he confessed that he still had never seen Pemberley, he found himself in good company, because Elizabeth and Margaret could boast of the same. Thus, he was able to ask them more about their lives in the South, which both women were willing to discuss with activity.

Elizabeth dominated the conversation, but it was not out of a disrespect to Margaret. It was merely because Elizabeth had four sisters, and therefore, more tales to tell.

With Margaret, she was unable to be more verbose from

her own nature and character. Also, she had much to reflect on.

She and Thornton were so very different.

But he wanted to understand her.

And by all logic, he had a right for her to try and understand him.

She was willing to try again, while accepting that something had changed between them. She found that she could no longer hold him in contempt. She never fully despised him, but nor did she ever accept him. Now, she had to confront, more than ever, that he was a part of her life. Whether she liked it or not. Therefore, it was best to let the matters unfold as they would. And respect him, even when they were at odds with each other.

Chapter 12

The Life You Save May Be Your Own

K itty and Rasby had constantly proven themselves to be a complex sort of duo, and their schemes always revolved around a camaraderie that few people had seldom experienced. Therefore, since they had both arranged to always have the same days off from work, they had planned to take a tour with Colonel Fitzwilliam and Mr. Bell throughout the outer parts of Milton, for there was some of the city that they had still not seen.

Mr. Bell, being an older man who enjoyed the company of younger people, looked forward to the outing, especially since he could entertain the lot of them. Colonel Fitzwilliam was able to be spared from his duties. However, Plato was shackled down to his position and could not attend. Thus, Colonel Fitzwilliam and Mr. Bell arrived at Frances Street, in all its squalor, to retrieve the two ladies who had packed a meal for them all to have a picnic together along the Milton green.

"The sooner you lot marry those sisters, the better," Mr. Bell said to Colonel Fitzwilliam when they approached the house, "the ladies need to be saved from this situation. They remain out here for too long, and the bad air might take them before the bad meat at the butcher's does."

"Where do these infernal butchers get their meat from here?" Colonel Fitzwilliam asked. "It's like they dip it in poison."

"One of the many reasons that I miss the South. Food may not be as flavorful as other parts of the world, but at least I know it will not kill me."

"There is only one problem," Colonel Fitzwilliam said.

"What is that, pray tell?"

"What will become of Rasby? When I take Kitty from here, Rasby might feel the loss."

"Oh, she will. She is a strong creature and could find her way on her own. However, I have another suggestion."

"What?"

"Take her with you."

Colonel Fitzwilliam looked at Mr. Bell as he knocked on the door.

"I cannot maintain two ladies in my household," Colonel Fitzwilliam said, "Sir, I have not the money, to be plain and frank about it."

"I don't propose that. It is just that I don't think it's right that both ladies be separate from each other. Rasby knows how to work. Find some way to have her assist the regiment. After all, she can be a part of the wandering company that you all have. She knows how to do laundry as well. And she needs protection. Now more than ever. Think on that."

The door opened and Kitty appeared, looking flustered as Rasby was behind her, putting the food in the baskets.

"Sorry for the delay in opening the door," She offered, taking Colonel Fitzwilliam's hand, and pulling him inside, with him smiling at her eagerness. "There was a clothing malfunction on our part."

"It was my doing," Rasby said, closing the basket, "My petticoat burst in the back and Kitty had to pin it closed."

Standing back, she twirled around.

"But good as new!" she declared.

"Better than new, my dear," Mr. Bell said, taking her hand, "you both look radiant."

"We packed a good meal," Rasby said, by way of thanking him. "We managed to find one butcher who found a good roast."

"A good roast in Milton? Now that is some kind of miracle."

Mr. Bell clapped his hands together.

"Now, when we reach Harley Street, I arranged for us to be met by some cabs. It will take us to the best spots to begin our excursion."

"I heard of a delightful prospect near the Canals," Colonel Fitzwilliam offered, "We can begin our excursion there and eat when we find a lovely spot."

The company agreed to this and set out for their casual stroll about Milton's outer areas...completely unaware of the crisis that they were about to face.

When they arrived a quarter of a mile away from the Canals, the cabs were paid, and Mr. Bell arranged for them to return in a couple hours' time.

"A happy thought," Kitty said, "planning ahead."

"When you reach a certain age, planning everything becomes as common and unconscious as breathing," Mr. Bell said, taking Rasby's arm, while Colonel Fitzwilliam took Kitty's arm, carrying the basket in his other hand. "Well, this invitation was a delightful surprise. It was the perfect way of my time ending in Milton."

"Ending?" Colonel Fitzwilliam asked. "Does that mean that you are leaving?"

"Yes, sadly, I must return back to Oxford and getting on with my studies and classes."

"You're leaving us?" Kitty asked.

"But that's a very sudden sort of decision, isn't it?" Rasby asked, a little anxious. Despite him being twice her age, Mr. Bell's company was immortal. He didn't give off airs, nor did he ever exude anything else but an easy conscience with a welcoming nature.

"All this concern for me leaving," Mr. Bell said, chuckling, "this is enough to make an old Oxford Academic almost giddy. Well, as giddy as an Oxford Academic can be."

They all laughed at his comment, but it soon died away when they remembered the prospect of his leaving them behind.

"The truth is that I have been neglecting my work," Mr. Bell continued, "for the pleasures of life. Usually when I come up here, it is a brief visit, simply to oversee that my properties are all in order. Then I return back to London. But this is one time where I stayed too long, out of selfish reasons. You brought congenial society to Milton, and it made me loathe to leave."

"You flatter us," Kitty responded.

"Flattery is an older man's refuge, but not this time. You lot are a set of young people who want an old man around. I shall not forget that."

Rasby was about to open her mouth and say something charming, when she was distracted by a familiar sight.

"Wait, is that Boucher?"

They all turned and saw Boucher a distance away from

them, across the field, headed toward the Canal. His posture was bent, he was evidently exhausted, and he was walking around as if he was a forlorn child, cast out onto a rocky precipice without family, connection, or sustenance. In fact, from what Kitty saw, he was terribly thin and unhealthy.

"He's probably hiding out here, ever since he was cast out," Kitty informed them.

"What do you mean by cast out?" Colonel Fitzwilliam asked.

"Boucher was the one who led the riot on Marlborough Mills. He didn't expect there to be any violence, perhaps, but he started it all the same. When that happened, the committee men shunned him, and all abandoned him. Well, in truth, it's worse. They shut him out. No one will speak to him or associate with him from now on, and none of the masters will hire him. That's what Nicholas Higgins told me."

"Good god," Mr. Bell stated, appalled, "he's been practically exiled then?"

"Yes, he was. And now look at him."

They all could not tear their eyes from him as they watched him traverse across the grounds and further along the canals.

"You think he's headed back to wherever he's hiding out," Colonel Fitzwilliam asked.

"I don't know," Kitty said, "but I wonder what could take him out here. There's no place to sleep, and he must be starving. After all, look at him."

All of them marked Boucher's progression, with four different reactions.

Mr. Bell was silently disgruntled that the committee men would be as heartless as the masters enough to permanently shun a man.

Kitty was thinking of Mrs. Boucher and how she could finally tell her where Boucher was.

Colonel Fitzwilliam was empathetic for the poor creature who walked along, feeling his good fortune once more. Often, he had lamented being born the second son and inheriting none of his father's estate. But now, when seeing real destitution before him, it put his life into a much sharper perspective. When all things were considered, his life was not so terrible.

The last reaction belonged to Raspberry. And her input on the matter was nuanced, woeful, and she was worried.

When seeing Boucher's hunched behavior, his aimless walking, his limping form, and dirty person, Rasby was apprehensive. The expression on Boucher's face gave all the indication of a familiar horror, of mischief being planned and soon attempted, of the road that led between life and the great unwinding of it all.

"He's going to do something awful," Rasby sensed, "I know it."

"What do you mean?" Mr. Bell asked.

"I know it sounds irrational, but I've seen that sort of emotional state before. I can't explain it, but I feel that something awful is about to happen. We have to follow him."

Rasby took a few steps and realized that no one was following her. Turning back, she saw how bewildered they looked. She was not surprised at all, for she must have sounded positively baffling.

"I know it sounds strange, but I think he is about to do a harm to himself. At the very least, let's try and get him back home to his wife."

Colonel Fitzwilliam walked up to her, looked beyond, at Boucher's appearance and tried to assess what she did. Suddenly the soldier-side of himself lit from within and he grew into being a man of action.

"I don't know if he plans to harm himself, but usually mischief follows such men when they are lumbering around like that. We'll follow him but not get too close. Come then."

They followed Boucher, and the more that they did so, the more they saw how he had regressed into a very miserable sort of creature. He was practically dragging himself, weakened from fatigue, restlessness, and starvation. His clothes were dirty and sagged loosely about him. The hounds of depravation hung about his expression and his hair was uncombed and fell about his face without care.

The more they followed, the more they pitied.

The more they pursued, the more certain they were that they were being led to something awful.

Either Boucher was leading them to some miserable place that he slept in, to a place where he would cause problems, or bestow the problem onto himself. They knew the road they were walking down would not be pleasant.

But they couldn't look away. Whether it was through curiosity or compassion, their feet carried them onward, till at last, they turned behind a building and saw Boucher crouched along the Canal that was just beyond Ashley Factory.

Boucher was all alone as he removed his shoes and dipped his feet into the canal.

"What's he doing?" Raspy gasped.

"Oh, he is bathing," Mr. Bell said, "and we intrude."

"But he can't get clean in that water. It's filled with purple dye from the dyeing vats that go into the canal. The dye is pushed into the water, and it turns the water purple."

"Boucher would know that," Kitty uttered, coming up behind Rasby. Slowly she began to share Rasby's suspicions. "He wouldn't bathe in there."

"No," Rasby confirmed, "he would not do that for any reason."

Boucher continued to move his feet in the water, every now and again removing them and seeing the progression of the dye against his pale white skin. Dipping his hand into the discolored water he ran his fingers back and forth in the drink, cupped his hand in the water and raised it up to his face.

"Do not drink it, man," Mr. Bell whispered, leaning over Rasby and staring at Boucher, enthralled by the spectacle of watching a man who was at the end of all hope. The perversity of the situation should have rendered it to be a pitiful spectacle where one would wish to look away, but that was not the case. Rather, seeing humanity pushed to the brink of all possibility and falling into a downward path is actually a striking image and the viewer cannot look away. Deep within Kitty, Rasby, Mr. Bell and the Colonel, they all did not know how their attention was so much seized because they felt a connection to Boucher. For there, within their bosoms was a despair that everyone shares from time to time. As such, to see their inner display in another person, and to see it so outwardly displayed, creates an unspoken connection. A binding tie.

No matter what Boucher had done, they knew that he felt sorry for the part he took in the riot.

His reduced circumstances also indicated that he had paid for his foolishness. Therefore, since he had been rightly reprimanded, there seemed no more room was needed for hatred and resentment. Fortune had punished him enough.

All took a sigh of relief when Boucher did not drink the dyed water. Rather, he kept pouring it back into the canal.

Then he would fill his palm up with water again, raise it up and watch it as it poured through his fingertips.

He repeated this action again and again.

Each time, he found a strange fascination with the water's progress. Eventually, he began to start muttering things to himself, another indication of how far he had sunk.

Though they were a distance away, Rasby focused on Boucher's eyes.

She saw it, in his gaze.

He was watching the water too keenly.

He was studying its strength, and marveling in the science of it.

She looked deeper.

Keener.

His expressions became more apparent to her, and she knew. She knew precisely what was in his mind.

"He is going to drown himself," Rasby gasped. "Boucher is going to drown himself."

———

Rasby's words could not have come sooner than she had anticipated.

As soon as all the water had dripped in Boucher's hand, his intent was set.

The moment of decision had come.

Standing up, Boucher looked even more deeply into the drink that was below him.

"Rasby," Mr. Bell whispered. "How deep is the water in there?"

"Not deep enough to drown in."

The silence hung about them like weights on their shoulders.

Each second was filled with a dreadful anticipation. Now they all shared the knowledge and knew what Boucher had been intending.

Leaning forward, he fell into the water and the purple seemed to fold in around him as he sunk down below.

The water crashed over his person and soon he disappeared into the shallow pool.

Now it all had been confirmed.

Boucher was trying to commit suicide.

At first, they waited for him to come to the surface. When he didn't, Kitty shouted, and Colonel Fitzwilliam removed his cloak and coat.

All of them ran forward, but Colonel proved to be the fastest of the four. Sprinting ahead of them, he reached the canal, dashed into the water, and found Boucher's body as Boucher was determined to press himself against the bottom of the canal and let the water fill his lungs.

Seeing Boucher's body at the bottom, Colonel Fitzwilliam reached down and began to pull Boucher out.

When Kitty and Rasby reached the water's edge, they remained there as Colonel Fitzwilliam was greeted with no struggle. He pulled Boucher from below, and both men reached the full surface.

Boucher's eyes were closed, and his body was limp in Colonel Fitzwilliam's arms.

"We're too late, dear god," Mr. Bell said, having finally reached the ladies.

"No, we're not," Colonel Fitzwilliam insisted, rolling Boucher over on his back, laying him flat against the ground, and opening Boucher's mouth wide. "There's something that I learned when an officer accidentally drowned when we were being shipped to France. He needs oxygen and to get it pumping in his lungs. Kitty and Rasby, take out your fans and begin to fan against his lips. It will help him get air into his mouth.

The ladies did as they instructed and fanned against Boucher's mouth as Colonel Fitzwilliam bent over Boucher, in a position where his feet were against either side of Boucher's hips. Next, he grabbed Boucher by the waist of his pants and began to lift him up by his midsection. Then he would lower it back to the ground.

He lifted up Boucher's midsection again. Then lowered it back down. This circular motion of Boucher's stomach was the mimic of how the lungs took in air.

"It doesn't always work," Colonel Fitzwilliam admitted, through frustrated teeth, "but we have to keep doing this. Keep pushing the air into him."

Together, Kitty, Rasby and Colonel Fitzwilliam repeated their actions. The more they did so, the more that the Colonel became desperate.

"For godsakes, man!" he cried. "Breathe! Get up and breathe. Breathe!"

The seconds counted down.

All hope was lost.

Then came a sharp gasp!

A desperate and intense breath of air!

Life into the lungs that stopped moving.

Air into the blood.

Eyes fluttering open.

Another gasp for breath.

Boucher was awake.

Boucher was alive.

When he came to, his face was discolored from some purple on it, but when his eyes opened, he cried out.

"Am I gone? Is this hell or heaven?"

"Neither, mate," Colonel Fitzwilliam said, "do you expect us to be here if it were?"

"I'm alive."

"Alive and somewhat whole," Mr. Bell replied, calming down, "much due to the efforts of your three saviors here. I was just an observer."

Boucher suddenly cried.

"Yer should have left me," he declared, "I shouldn't be here anymo'. The world hates me. The world hates me!"

"Oh, shut up, will you!" Kitty cried, hugging him around the neck. This sudden act of affection disarmed Boucher. Not only was it a surprise because he was wet and must have looked atrocious, but because it was special. It was the first true sign of affection that he had felt in days. The weeks had lumbered on in a quick succession of failures on his part.

Failures to stand up to the committee when it doomed his wife and children to starvation.

Failures to the strike when he inspired the riot that would go on to attack Marlborough Mills and the women who defended the Thorntons.

Failure to his wife.

Failure to his children.

He was nothing to anyone.

And now, here at the end of the life that he tried to end, he was given acceptance.

The very raft to a man who had been drowning in more ways than one. He clung to the embrace. Even before his mind could process what kindness was, his body grasped for it. Throwing his arms around Kitty was instinctive, to the point where it awakened Colonel Fitzwilliam's protective side and he had the instinct to throw Boucher's arms off her. His rational side, however, won out and he kept his arms at his side, watching to make sure that Boucher's hands did not roam anywhere that was improper.

Eventually, the instinct to cling to affection bestowed upon Boucher was compiled with the logic that he was saved by two ladies who he had caused harm to. Kitty and Rasby were there for him in the same manner that he had not been there for them at some point.

"I'm sorry," He urged her to believe, "I'm so sorry. Rasby, Kitty, I..."

"Hush now," Kitty urged him to believe, "we know."

Putting her fan away, Rasby leaned down with the picnic basket.

"Boucher," Rasby suggested, "I think it's time you ate something."

Boucher's eyes drained of color, but all the emotions of appreciation and gratitude filled them instead.

"How di' yer know?" he asked. "How did you know?"

"Your face. It was hungry for something." Rasby looked at Mr. Bell. "I think we need to get him into some dry clothes before he catches cold." Rasby pulled out the blankets that they were going to use for the picnic. "Till then, Boucher, take off your jacket, waistcoat and shirt."

"Be quick about it man," Colonel Fitzwilliam ordered, and that did the trick. Removing his clothing, Boucher felt a little insecure as Rasby wrapped the blankets around him.

Kitty looked to where he had placed his shoes, walked over to them, picked them up and Boucher put them back on.

"Come," Kitty said, "we'll take you back to Frances Street."

"I can't face my wife like this," Boucher wept. "First I was too weak to support her, and now I was even too weak to take my life."

"Ah, a double shame," Rasby said, out of patience, taking out some roast and bread as she handed it to him. "Yes, that is truly the *worst* thing, isn't it?"

Boucher ate the food greedily.

"Yer mock me."

"Yes, I do."

"Good," he responded, "I like bein' mocked by yer right now. For some reason, it gives me the feelin' that someone cares for me."

They gave him a little more food before they all stood up and walked along the canal. When doing so, Boucher took one last look at the water, where he had been intent to drown himself in.

The purple hue continued rushing along the stream.

'A shame on it!' Boucher thought savagely. 'It flows along, as if nothing ever happened. As if I was not abou' to give me lifeforce to it, where it took everythin' from me, and gave nothin' in return. Well, it has my pride now. It shall have to be content with tha'.'

He stared at it for too long and Mr. Bell seemed to sense what was going on in Boucher's mind.

"Don't worry, Boucher," Mr. Bell said, "nor be afraid. It can't do anything to hurt you anymore. Just let it be."

With an optimistic heaviness, Boucher looked away from the water that was meant to be his grave, sighed out and walked away with the company.

Wrapping the blankets even more around himself,

Boucher allowed himself to be guided wherever they would take him.

"I don' know much Shakespeare," Boucher said, "I was never given the education for all that, yer know? But there's somethin' that I do reckon I recall. It was a line that said, 'If life be short, then shame will be too long'."

"That was from 'Henry V'," Mr. Bell answered, "not one of my favorite monarchs, by far—I quite detested how he treated any cities he captured in France, and especially his actions at the Battle of Rouen. What he did to the women and children there was villainous—but still one of my favorite Shakespeare plays."

"Well," Boucher said, "I appreciate all that yer done, with savin' my life and all, but it's the reverse. With my life bein' longer, the shame will be longer, yer see? If I come back, with them all knowin' I tried to kill meself and not bein' successful, they will laugh at me, on top of jus' ignorin' me."

"They won't if they never know," Colonel Fitzwilliam replied. "We'll make up a story."

Boucher looked at him, through glazed over eyes.

"Yer would do that, for me?"

"Why not?"

"Because I never did anythin' to deserve owin' yer a favor."

"I never asked for one, now, did I?"

"No. I don't suppose yer did."

When they reached the nearest field, Mr. Bell groaned.

"What is it?" Rasby asked.

"I ordered the cab to pick us up in two hours' time," Mr. Bell said.

"Oh!" they all said together, realizing that they were

forced to remain there for another hour and a half until their transportation arrived.

"Well, that just goes to prove it," Mr. Bell conceded, "that when mankind makes plans, god laughs."

"Well, best to get on with the picnic then," Colonel Fitzwilliam said, "and put the food on our laps."

"It will give us time enough to come up with a plan," Kitty said to Boucher.

They all sat down and had to ignore any grass stains that might accumulate on their clothing.

When they laid out the food, Boucher began to eat voraciously.

"When is the last time you had a proper meal, if you don't mind me asking?" Colonel Fitzwilliam asked Boucher.

Boucher lowered the bread and roast that he was about to swallow, and he stared ahead.

"I... I don't remember."

This acknowledgement made the rest of the company look between each other, flabbergasted.

Suddenly, Boucher began to chuckle sadly.

"Isn't tha' odd? To not remember the last time yer ate somethin' whole. To not remember?" Boucher turned to Kitty and Rasby, with imploring eyes. "Does me wife and childer eat? Higgins said he be lookin' after them before he drove me away. But I know that yer both care. Tell me that they are eatin' properly."

"They are," Rasby assured him, very aware what he was referring to. "Your children are, we promise."

"They must hate me."

"None of that," Mr. Bell stressed, "hate yourself only when you are certain to have full reason. In the meantime, softly *softly*."

Boucher continued to eat his full, wondering if this meal was the first of his new fortunes after being given a new life, or the last of his fortunes.

Chapter 13

The Rapture of Returns

When we returned to Frances Street, Charlotte, Margaret, and I entered my home to the most surprising sight.

"Boucher!"

Sitting at our table, was Boucher, covered in blankets. Rasby was sitting in a corner, washing his clothes in one of our washbasins. When she finished, Boucher would ring them out in the water and hang them on the dry rack.

Will wonders never cease?

When seeing us, Boucher stood up nervously, covering himself even more thoroughly.

"Miss Bennet!" Boucher cried. "Miss Hale and..."

"Oh," I began, at a loss of how to fully proceed. After all, I had an obviously naked man covered in blankets in our parlor. Our only parlor at that. "Forgive me, Boucher, this is my dear friend from Hertfordshire, Charlotte Lucas from Lucas Lodge. Charlotte, this is Mr. Boucher, the husband of the woman you met earlier."

Oh, this was so awkward. Boucher had to bow his head

to Charlotte. Charlotte was aware of the lack of contents under his blankets. Or our blankets, as I should say.

"Nice to meet yer, Miss Lucas," Boucher said.

"Nice to make your acquaintance, Mr. Boucher. I had the fortune of being introduced to your wife and your children. They are a lovely set, and you ought to be proud."

"Thank yer. Whether or not they are proud of me is another story," he said, by way of a joke. Yet, considering his circumstances, the scene did paint an accurate picture.

"Before you go thinking it, Charlotte," Kitty said as she began to pour coffee for all of us, "entertaining men in blankets is not a usual custom in our parlor."

"Yes," I furthered, "it's not."

"I fear that I paint a very poor portrait o' things, I reckon," Boucher observed.

"On the contrary," I said, "I am dying to know what led to this set of events."

"As am I," Margaret said, "before that, Boucher, where have you been? Your wife and children didn't know what became of you."

"We have a problem before we get to that explanation," Kitty observed, "Charlotte is still confused."

We looked at Charlotte, who was evidently curious about what Boucher meant to us.

"I know that Mr. Boucher took part in the riot on Marlborough Mills, and that your family are in destitution."

"My sins are more than that, I reckon," Boucher said, "my family are aroun' the corner, and even they don't know that I am here."

"Your wife and children don't know that you are merely a few houses down from them," Margaret repeated, "but surely they will find out from anyone who saw you come here."

Boucher looked ashamed.

"I didn' think of that."

"And yet, you did not go to them first. Boucher, what reason do you have?"

"There is a reason for it," Kitty said for him, "there is a complication on the matter."

"First, Miss Lucas," Boucher said, "I have done more than what yer know. I didn' jus' take part in the riot at Marlborough Mills, but I was the one who incited it. I was also the one who's actions led to the Miss Bennets and Miss Pitcher gettin' brutally attacked. That led to us attackin' the Irish. And I'm also the one who everyone blames for ruinin' the strike."

He took a sip of his coffee and stared into the fire.

"Who ruined many things. I didn't mean for it, yer understand? I never wanted the ladies here to get hurt. It was not what I wanted."

"I'm sure that you didn't."

"Boucher," Margaret said, sitting down next to him at the table, "we forgave you for that. You were starving, heartbroken and desperate. There were things worthy of regret, but we are willing to give you another chance."

"Yes, I reckon yer are," Boucher responded, chuckling sadly as he swallowed his drink, "but not the rest of the world. What 'bout them, eh? What 'bout the rest of the world? What 'bout those who go to church on Sunday, and don' know what any of the sermons mean? What of the world, Miss Hale? It's not like yer lot."

Margaret turned and looked at me. Kitty and Rasby did the same thing. That was when it occurred to me of the responsibility that went with my name and my station in the group.

I was the one that they all turned to and expected to have

an answer. It was my own fault; I had a habit of taking charge of things, to the point where I potentially had set myself up as the head figure of our set.

Now I knew what Darcy must have felt every time that Mr. Bingley had sought him for advice. Therefore, I had to take my time and choose my judgments carefully. After all, it was so easy to give everyone the wrong advice and to lead them astray.

Sitting down, I drank a bit of my coffee.

"Boucher," I began, "it's time to tell Margaret and I where you have been. I need to know everything and—"

We were interrupted when we heard a key turning in the door. It opened and Jane entered, followed by Maria. Maria had evidently said something funny because Jane entered laughing.

All mirth died, however, when they cast their eyes on Boucher, draped in blankets.

Delightful! Just delightful! Now Boucher had two more women looking upon his embarrassed form. How much humiliation could the man take before he keeled over in exasperation?

"Maria," Jane began, trying to placate the situation, "This is Mr. Boucher, our neighbor. Boucher, this is Maria Lucas."

"Of Lucas Lodge?" Boucher said, looking in between she and Maria.

"Yes," Charlotte said, "She is my younger sister, sir."

"I assumed as such. Yer and she look alike. Bein' refined as well, and all. Good day, Miss Maria."

"Good day, Mr. Boucher."

"I can assure yer, I'm harmless."

"Before a long series of explanations begin," Kitty said as Rasby moved the washbasin, "I should tell you, Maria, that we do not usually entertain bare-skinned people in our parlor."

Rasby chuckled and we all turned to her.

"Sorry," Rasby said, "but I'm just wondering how many times you will have to say that."

"I know." Kitty rolled her eyes. "I wonder that too."

Together, Kitty and Rasby carried the water from the washbasin outside, dumped the dirty water in the street and came back inside.

"Well," I said, pouring Maria some coffee, "now we can begin, can't we? Boucher, go ahead." I looked at him, informative. "After all, it's only a matter of time before Nicholas knows you are here as well."

Boucher's eyes widened.

"He wants to kill me, doesn't he?"

I took a sip of my coffee.

"Perhaps."

Everyone looked at me. I couldn't help but chuckle. Dear lord, there really was a hint of wickedness in me.

Boucher told us everything that had happened to him since he ruined the strike.

From the devastation he felt when he saw Margaret get hit by the clog, to hearing that we all had been attacked when defending the Irish.

Then he told us about the edict that was passed by the committee of it being decreed that no one would speak to him or talk to him. He was entirely cast out by everyone. When he went to Hampers and Thornton's to get his job back—even admitting that he forsook his union dues—he was refused and could not earn any money. This led to him becoming depressed and despondent, as was natural. What was chilling was how he described his exile.

"I just walked," Boucher said, still looking into the fire and away from our inquisitive eyes. It made sense and it was easier for both parties. After all, it is easier to tell a story when you don't have to see the eyes of your audience. Just like it was easier to tell a story when you didn't have to stare into the eyes of the listener.

The firelight danced across his face and the flames lit up his eyes.

"And I walked some more," he continued, "and I kept walkin' and walkin'. It's always frightenin' when yer walk so far and yer have nowhere to go. And no one to return to. Yer marry a woman, but yer can't return to her. She is guilty by association with yer. At least when yer are gone, she can be pitied. But while yer stay, she will be a creature of scorn an' spite. That scornful look will be placed on yer. The world and she will cease to look on yer at all. How could I put my children through all tha'? No father could. So, instead, yer just walk and yer keep walkin'. Then yer get hungry, and yer stomach eats away at itself. The water is disgustin' to drink. And the world be lookin' so terribly ugly. Yer then realize that yer ain't worth anythin' alive. Maybe yer might be worth more if yer dead. Yer become less of a burden and a blight to them all. A bitter pill it is, but it is what it is. And then, when the hunger has gotten to yer, when the thirst has made yer lips crust o'er, yer don't see death as the oblivion that yer used to view it as. Yer see it as a release. As a way out. So, I found my way out."

He closed his eyes when he said this, and we all felt enthralled by the story. We knew he wasn't lying. After all, Kitty, the Colonel and Mr. Bell were there to see him die and then be resurrected. If there was any attempt to find his suicide to be cowardly, then it had been quite done away.

When he was saved by the Colonel, Kitty and Rasby, the gentlemen brought them back here, then departed for their homes. This left Boucher time for them all to decide what was best for us all to do.

"One thing is for certain," I finalized, "this must be a secret, like Colonel Fitzwilliam suggested. Boucher must never be known to have attempted suicide."

"But if your wife knew about it," Jane pointed out, "then she would feel sorry for your situation."

"No, she might not," I said, "no offense, Boucher, but his wife would find his actions deplorable. Especially since he was not successful. Now he has to face those he had intended to leave behind." I sighed. "Boucher, I didn't mean it like that. I only meant that they would see it in such a fashion."

"I understand. And yer right, miss. She would see it tha' way."

"So," Maria said, "we can't let this event leave us?"

"Agreed," Kitty finalized, "it can never leave this room."

Suddenly, we heard banging on our front door. This made us all jump in terror.

"Dear god!" Kitty cried, frustrated, "what is it now?"

Jane went to the window and looked out of it.

"It's Nicholas!"

We all turned to Boucher, and he looked as if he had been slapped with a hot iron.

"Sorry for being ignorant," Maria requested, "but why does everything seem to be so wrong right now?"

"We should take Boucher upstairs," Rasby suggested, "Nicholas is still angry from losing Bessy. He will take it out on Boucher."

"I know," I said, going to the door, "but Nicholas probably already knows that Boucher is here. That's why he's banging so loudly. Sorry, Boucher, but there is no time for being a coward about things."

I opened the door and stood in the middle of it. Facing me, in his fury, was Nicholas Higgins. Fortunately, two could play that game. I stared at him with such a cold fury that his eyes transformed from wrath to subtle uncertainty. I don't think he expected to be met with the same level of stubbornness.

"Nicholas!" I hissed. "What in the name of Mary Queen of Scots do you think you are doing by banging on my door in such a fashion? Apologize right now."

"I heard that—"

"Nicholas, I *said* apologize right now and be a gentleman when you come in here, or don't come at all. And quite frankly, I've had a long day, and you are depriving me of my chance to jump into a bath at the nearest possible opportunity. And whatever you are about to demand, I have no answer for those who do not respect my door, and if you want to know something, you need only ask politely."

My little speech had unnerved him to such a degree that Nicholas Higgins was a little taken aback and didn't know how to begin to speak.

"Well," I insisted, "speak your words up sharp, man. Or be forever standing in the doorway."

"I didn' mean to offend," Nicholas said, removing his hat to be respectful.

"I know you didn't. You are clearly just angry, and maybe you have reason to be. But I'm not in the mood to suffer angry men to be vehement at my doorway; it never bodes well for the chinaware within. So, what is it?"

Nicholas's eyes turned dark again, with ill intent in them.

"I heard that Boucher was here."

"Truly, that's what you heard?"

"Yes."

"Lord, how quickly the world always turns to spying to get its pleasures in life. Can no one ever mind their business anymore?"

"Not to be rude, Miss Elizabeth, but I don' think the world has ever minded its own business."

"Fair point. Yes, Boucher is here. If you want to come in here to speak to him, then you can. I'll even let you express your disappointment, but you must let him explain himself. You must not blame him for what happened to Bessy, nor take your anger out on him for that incident. And you can't be cruel. Tell him what you feel but also give him the right to speak. Agreed?"

Nicholas groaned.

"What kind of world do we live in when I have to take orders from a woman?" He asked himself, but the offense was keenly felt.

"What did you say?" I asked, rhetorically. Oh, the feeling of venom. "Well, now you cannot come in. Have a delightful evening knowing that you brought your sleepless night on yourself."

"Miss Elizabeth, please, I meant no offense."

"Doesn't matter if you didn't mean it. You gave it, nonetheless. If you can't take orders from a woman in her own doorway, then you aren't fit to be seen. Make up your mind, man. What will it be?"

He ground his teeth.

"Yer don' know how hard it is for me to resist stranglin' him by the throat."

"I know. That's why I warned you."

He sighed.

"Very well. I have offended and I will make it right by obeyin'. That's a lot, comin' from me."

"I know it is."

I stepped aside.

"And wipe your shoes on the rug," I told him. "They are filthy."

After wiping his feet, Nicholas Higgins entered and saw Boucher standing up from where he sat, still covered in blankets.

Nicholas took one look at him and became venomous again.

"What the devil?"

Kitty sighed.

"You're going to have to say it again, aren't you?" Rasby asked.

"Yes."

"We don't usually entertain bare-skinned men in our parlor," Jane, Kitty and I said together.

"Then explain this," Nicholas cried, staring venomously at Boucher. "What sort of mischief have yer undergone now? Bad enough yer ruined everythin' and then abandon yer family, but now yer ruinin' these ladies' reputation."

Boucher stood up, preparing to defend himself, but he was in such a pitiable state that he would have made a poor defense. Also, I was quite tired from the events of the day, and I wanted this resolved as quickly as I could.

"And that's where we need your help, Nicholas," I

stressed, "and it would be best for me to explain. Boucher's clothes are wet because he saved my sister, Lydia's life."

When I spoke, everyone looked at me in alarm. Nicholas was the only one who was innocently surprised. The rest of them were watching me as I was about to unroll a list of fibs.

"My sister, Lydia, was wondering along the canal with some friends. She took a tumble and fell in. Boucher was hiding out in that area. When he saw her fall in, he dove in to assist her. As gratitude for his heroics, we invited him to return to Frances Street where we gave him a warm meal and washed his clothes for him."

"What?" Nicholas asked.

"It's true. Isn't it, Boucher?"

Nicholas turned to Boucher, to confirm the truth of this.

In Boucher's eyes was a 'Elizabeth, how can I commit to such a lie?' look.

All that was left was for me to return it with a 'be quiet and just agree already' look.

Boucher closed his eyes, shutting them away from the lie he was about to assign himself to. His face ashamed, he nodded and confirmed my deception.

Nicholas rubbed his lips, trying to make sense of what he was hearing. Turning away, he walked to our fireplace and leaned against it, staring into the flames.

"Well, I'll be buggered." Walking up to Nicholas, I touched his shoulder.

"Sometimes, people can surprise you, eh?" I asked, light-hearted.

"Yea, I s'pose they can. Well, I s'pose very few people only have bad or good in them."

"Yes, you have now been faced with the duality of mankind. And all its infinite alarming wonders." I leaned in close. "You still have a hard time looking at Boucher, don't you?"

"Yes," he whispered back, "now more than ever."

"It's understandable. You don't have to look at him now but do it when you are ready. But we need your help now."

"What can I do?" he asked, grudgingly.

"He may have wronged both you and us, but he saved our sister. We can't forget that. And maybe, no one else should. Tell people, Nicholas. Tell them that he saved Lydia. It will help his wife and children a lot. Do it for them, if not for anyone else."

Nicholas rolled his head, in frustration.

"I'll think 'bout it," he said.

"How long will you think about it?" I asked.

He turned to me, his eyes like stone. I returned it, unafraid.

He groaned.

"Must you tear my heart out by being a woman, Miss Lizzy?"

"Yes. It's what I do. Bessy's gone, and it hurts you. It ought to hurt. We all miss her. If you do this for me, I will thank you. The committee needs to pardon Boucher. It's his family's only chance."

"For the family. Aye, I can do that, at least."

Nicholas looked at Boucher.

"Well, mate. Yer have yer better side now. Be best to keep it."

With that, Nicholas left.

When Nicholas Higgins was gone, Boucher almost wept.

"I can't commit to that," Boucher pleaded, "I can't have people praisin' me for somethin' that I never did."

"You have to," I said, "or you would make a liar out of

me. You are a villain to everyone right now. The only thing that could remedy that is to have you look like a hero."

"But it's all a lie."

"I know."

"But in circumstances like these," Kitty considered, "maybe the truth is not enough."

"I can't make this up to yer."

"Yes, you can," Jane stressed, going up to him and taking his hands in her own. "If you spend the rest of your life being better, being kind to us, and striving for a more peaceful way, a moral one, then you will have made it up to us."

"Can you do that, Boucher?" Margaret asked. "You must do it."

"I can," he answered, "I will."

"Good," I said, not wishing to be mean, but it had to be done, "because if not, I can always tell the truth."

"I understand," he said, simply. "I promise, yer will never have to."

"I know that I won't."

He leaned back, taking another sip of coffee. Opening his eyes again, he scanned over all of us.

His gaze turned to Kitty, to Rasby, to me, then Jane, Margaret, and lastly to Charlotte and Maria.

"There be kindness in yer eyes," he observed, "in each of yer eyes."

He leaned back.

"If I ha' been raised around such kindness, then I might have been different. Sometimes I even wonder if I ha' been born in the South. If I ha' been born in the South..."

"The South cannot make one better, because villains are everywhere," Margaret said, then she grew bashful. She had just spoken of a negative quality of the South. That was novel. "You can be better up here, in the North."

"That remains to be seen, Miss Hale. Yer may be a kind woman, but I have to find a life for meself. No matter how heroic yer are, even yer can't save me from the damage that I have done." He tapped Rasby's hand. "But yer saved me from everythin' else. I'll smile again, because of it."

A little while later, his clothes were dried by the fireplace, he put them on, and it was time for him to face his wife.

"I'll go with you," Kitty said, "I'll best explain it to your wife. Rasby, any chance that..."

"Don't worry," Rasby said, "I'll come with you. After all, we've got a story to keep to."

The two of them went off with Boucher, down the street. Despite the snippiness of the night air, all of us went to the doorway and watched as Boucher and the ladies walked to his door.

Retreating into himself, Boucher wrapped his arms around his body, as if he was protecting himself from what he was about to do.

"Is he really a coward?" Charlotte asked me. "Or doesn't have any nerve?"

"Yes," I answered, "he might be. But that's his flaw to get over. Hopefully, he will get over it."

They reached his door, and he knocked on it. He must have left his key there, so he waited till Mrs. Boucher opened it. There she was, holding her youngest child, when she stared back at him.

"Where?" She wept. "Where the devil have yer been?"

Suddenly, as if he was driven with a burst of passion, Boucher closed the space between them and kissed her savagely.

"That's what happens when you have a brush with

death, I suppose," Margaret uttered, "you must be given a breath of life."

"Yes," Jane said. "Now, come away from the door. We must not be seen spying."

We closed the door, but I couldn't help but spy them through a window.

Boucher was still kissing his wife, and she did not shy away.

Kitty and Rasby could only look away, waiting for the moment when they could turn back again.

Yet, husband and wife needed their moment.

Never would Mrs. Boucher know how close she was to becoming a widow.

Never would the children know that they had almost become half-orphaned.

Never would the truth be known that Boucher got sick of living and decided to end it all.

All they knew were deceptions that were meant to save a life and save a family.

I could live with that. Because I already had lived with that.

"Lizzy," Jane said, "come away from the window. Please."

I did so, leaving Boucher to his own counsel now. I had done enough.

Chapter 14

Unpleasant Conversations

Soon after Boucher's return home, it was time for Margaret to return to Crampton. I escorted her to the main street, to fetch a cab, and she was silent the whole way.

"You're quiet," I observed.

"Am I? I didn't notice."

"Yes, you did. Because you have been quieter than usual." But I knew her mind. I knew that she was unsettled, and maybe even angry with me. "You can be honest with me, Margaret. You know that I am unafraid when I fall short of your morality."

"Elizabeth..."

"You say my name. Now we are getting somewhere."

"You lied. You lied about what really happened."

"Yes, I did lie. That upsets you. We saved a man's life and his family."

"I know and that should make me happy. But you know how I feel about lying."

"Yes, I do. You detest it."

"Even when there's a good reason behind it, it still makes

189

me uncomfortable. I cannot change that. And what's more, I didn't speak out against it. Now I feel heartily sorry about that."

"Margaret, you are too severe upon yourself—like you are being severe to me."

"No, the truth means everything. If we start lying, to make heroes out of anyone, where does it end? Soon, life would be full of heroes who do nothing more amazing than the average flawed person."

"If we ruled the world, then I would fear any deception that we tried to pull, but as of right now, we are as uninfluential as the rest of mankind. I know that this is hard for you, so I'll let you think as you may. Besides, we have not done much, because Boucher needs a job."

"Yes, he does. Or he will still not be able to support his family."

"He used to work at Marlborough Mills. Will Thornton let him have his old post back? He didn't before, but maybe he might now."

"Thornton is against it," Margaret acknowledged, "unless..."

"Unless what?"

"Unless I asked him."

I was hoping she would consider that.

"That's good. Mrs. Boucher would appreciate that. I am aware that might be hard for you."

"It will, but as you say, I claim to care, so I ought to. Dear lord, how did I get caught up in such a situation?"

"Circumstances. They always rule our lives."

Margaret sighed as the cab rolled up alongside us.

"Elizabeth, I don't think I have the energy to continue on like this. Every day presents another conflict."

"I know. But I'm going to be gone soon. I can't help you make decisions anymore."

"I know," Margaret answered, "soon, I shall have to be making these decisions all on my own. I suppose I need the practice."

"Yes, you do. And you will be splendid. I believe in you."

"Well, if you do, then I suppose I ought to believe in myself."

"Your father needs you to do that. You are his strength, you know."

"Yes, I do know. That's the heaviest part of all."

She got into the cab and looked down at me.

"Tell Boucher that I will pay Mr. Thornton a visit tomorrow and see if he is interested in allowing Boucher to return."

"Thornton will be happy to see you. Be kind to him, but don't encourage him."

"I know. That's the difficult part."

"Give my regards to Mr. Hale and tell Mrs. Hale that we will visit her again very soon."

"She will like that. It cannot be long now," she replied, even heavier than the rest of the conversation.

The cab took off and carried Margaret back to Crampton. Woes awaited her there, just like woes awaited me back home. Oh well, best to get on with it.

Darcy, where are you? Be safe, beloved.

"You used me!" Lydia roared.

The next day had come, and since there was only one class that day at Granger Hall, I immediately went afterwards to visit Lydia and Denny at the regiment's head-quarters.

Denny was off, seeing to his duties, but Lydia was in their compartment, arranging the laundry. Happy to catch her alone, I explained Boucher's situation to her and the part I had her play in it—without her permission.

"I am sorry," I said, "it was a random act that I improvised in the suddenness of the moment."

Lydia's exclamation turned out not to be one of annoyance or resentment, but actually amusement. Naturally, giving into her comical side, she leaned her head back and laughed.

"You lied," she commented, "you lied to save Boucher, and then you used me for it. What a good joke."

"Well, I'm happy to see that you are not upset with me about it."

"Upset with you? Now why would I do that when there are so many other avenues to walk down?"

"I beg your pardon?"

"Eliza, you used me without my permission. Now mind you, there was no harm in it, and I am happy that I was able to help at all, even if in name only. I am not against being thought of or included in the tale, especially when it's so amusing. However, you did do it without my permission. That means you owe me a favor."

Seeing what she meant, I closed my eyes and groaned inwardly.

"Oh, I totally sabotaged myself, didn't I?" I questioned.

"Yes, you did," Lydia said, laughing. "Now you're in my debt."

"I really should have used Jane instead of you, shouldn't I have?"

"Yes, you should have. But, sadly for you, and happily for

me, that thought had not occurred to you. Oh, now this is a good feeling. Not just because it takes you from your lofty place of being the sister who is supposedly mentally superior than me, but also because it could help. After all, Denny and I would love to see Pemberley. Or it would be nice to get a gift of a few pounds every now and again. Being a soldier's wife is not the easiest thing, you know? Or a gift of a lovely gown. That sort of thing."

"Did I make a deal with the devil?"

"Never fear, Lizzy. My demands are not going to be extreme. You know that I'm merely teasing. Don't get me wrong, I will ask for help every now and again, especially since you are soon to be so very rich. But I will not let it strain you or take advantage. All I will ask is for a little help, once in a while. Besides, the help I ask for is merely the help that I would have asked you for *even if* you didn't owe me a favor."

That was true, the more that I thought about it.

Now that I was Darcy's fiancée, Lydia naturally would see the advantages for her side. And it did make sense. After all, what is family for?

Seeing that I really didn't have to worry, and that Lydia was playing a good joke at my expense, I felt my worries lessen. Lydia was a jester, not an abuser.

When returning home, I found Charlotte resting from her morning that she spent testing her notetaking skills at Granger Hall. The class we had attended was her first real test and I couldn't take notes for her.

Rather, Mr. Hanley was insistent that I do nothing but observe, which I did. Charlotte managed to write everything of vital importance, in notetaking form that was easy to read, thorough, and comprehensive. By the end of the class, Mr. Hanley was impressed.

Before we had left, he gave me another significant look before we had departed. Since I had a personal errand when seeking Lydia, I let Charlotte rest in my room, which she was eager to do. Between today's task, and yesterday's events, she was still exhausted, therefore it was easy to let her be while I went off and visited the regiment.

When I had returned, it was to seeing Rasby in the kitchen, making dough for bread and she was alone.

"Miss Lucas is still sleeping, and Kitty is upstairs taking a bath," She explained, "I told her that I would make some bread while she bathed, then I would take a bath afterwards."

"Understandable," I said, without any question in my voice. Rasby's treating our home like it was her second house was so natural at this point, that I barely ever questioned it.

I removed my coat, hat, and began to make some tea. The space in our kitchen was small, so we had to do a little bit of maneuvering while we each performed our task.

"Mr. Thornton came by to visit today," Rasby informed me.

"He did?"

"Yes. He wanted to inquire after you."

"Did he mention anything about Margaret going to see him?"

"No, he didn't. To be honest, he and I are not that comfortable around each other. Plato understands him, but he is too severe for me to ever know how to approach. I think he sensed that, because when he saw that you were not here, he went away directly."

"Don't take it personally," I offered, "Thornton doesn't

always know how to approach casual conversation. I think, because of his upbringing, he never found out how."

"I always wondered if maybe he wondered if I was ever fully worth talking to."

I prepared my teapot.

"You think so?" I asked. "Never mind, perhaps that is a foolish question. Sorry, I had never thought of it that way before. I cannot even pretend to know what revolves around the minds of others."

I poured the hot water into the teapot and stirred the tea into it.

"Want some?" I asked.

"Thank you, but no. Already had a cup."

"Does it bother you when others are uncomfortable around you?" I asked her, without any sense of shame or pretense. In fact, the way I said it, it sounded as if I might have been asking if 'are you enjoying the good weather that we have been having?'.

"I've learned to get used to it."

"Oh, come now," I said, wishing to know more. "That is not what I asked you. You are uncomfortable, admit it. There's no shame in it. I noticed it when you were introduced to Charlotte and Maria."

"Well, yes, if you must know."

"I would rather know. There's no point in us ignoring something that you might want to talk about."

"It's not that I want to talk about it. Truth is, we all hate to *have* to talk about it."

"I can see why. I would hate to talk about it. It is an awkward business, isn't it?"

"Yes, it is. And it always leads to me becoming angry."

"Well then, that's settled. You *need* to talk about it."

"You must understand that, I suppose, I got too complacent," she responded.

"What do you mean by complacent?"

"Well, I was so used to Kitty and the rest of you, that I forgot that anyone from the South would ever view me as different. After all, you didn't."

"We've given you a romantic idea of what the South is like, then."

"I know. Meeting the Lucases changed that perspective very quickly. I haven't been to the South in years, therefore, I thought that the change was significant."

I sat down and leaned back, thinking about the matter.

"I suppose, the South is like anywhere else in the world that has the great homes and sophisticated ideas: the pretenses of modern and superior thinking are felt too keenly. Put simply, because we are aware of our superior intellect, we know we are superior, and that leads to an inferior outlook on the rest of the world. Intelligence only works where there is a great deal of humility involved. But when it is not relegated to the proper recesses of our mind, it becomes like a sort of infection. Be wary of those people who are superior of mind and know it, that's my advice. Those sorts are so smart that they justify all illogical and malicious sorts of behavior. How do you think we justified chaining down your people for so long?"

When hearing me finally mention it, Rasby turned to me. I suppose we had been forgetting the subject for so long, that we never thought to approach it. It was not that we were ignoring talking about it—neither she nor I proved to be afraid to talk of things—I suppose it was just that we did not need to. But now, with the subject being forced upon us, now was as good a time as any to show our courage—to show our quality.

"The Trade was not an action of a dumb people who knew they were being ignorant," I furthered, "No. It was done by those who were considered educated and intelligent, and so they felt they had the right to justify anything. Well, it still is that way...in all parts of the world. My only wonder is that I am not certain if it will ever change."

"But you were not that way," Rasby insisted. "When we first met, you didn't seem to care about what I was."

I looked at her, unafraid and without any sense of guilt. Quite frankly, my guilt was not what she needed right now.

"Actually, that's not true," I confessed, simply and easily.

"What do you mean it's not true?" she asked, ceasing her needling the dough.

"I mean that when I did meet you, I was apprehensive. I was shocked, uncomfortable, and I wondered that any in my family associated with you."

When hearing this, Rasby merely flinched and blinked. She was perhaps frozen under the news of my barbarous initial reaction.

"You didn't show it," she observed.

"No, I didn't. Because, as far as first impressions go, it was like a quick wave: it came and went as quickly as the tide coming in and out. You see, I was raised to believe that we committed the worst crime to Africa, as well as to the Natives in America and Australia, and that we ought to praise ourselves for eventually putting an end to such a thing. But *it* still happened, and *it* can't be changed. When you've begun treating someone unequal, it's hard to fully remove the stain. It can be a hard habit to break. Just because we freed you doesn't mean that our instincts shift immediately, and we start treating you equally. We don't. We haven't. Like most of the world, I was given good principles but left to practice them in pride and conceit. I cannot change a habit and inclination that was engrained in me from when I was born. All I could do was identify the problem in me when it presented itself. I suppose that the only reason that I was able to overcome the beast of my worse side was for two reasons."

"What reasons would those be?"

"First, I met you already humbled. I had gone through experiences where my pride was knocked down and I knew that I had it in me to be wrong before, so it was easy to accept being wrong again. Second, it was Kitty."

"Kitty," Rasby asked, her eyes lighting up a little in hearing that her best friend had a hand in my trans-formation.

"Yes. When I met you, Kitty acted as if your presence in her life was nothing short of comfortable camaraderie. She didn't care for your difference. Therefore, I didn't care for it either."

"Her relationship with me rubbed off on you?"

"Love is like hate; it's easy to spread it. She loved you, so I was able to ignore my prejudices and see why she did. But simply, in that regard, I got lucky. I'd apologize for my first impression, but something tells me that it doesn't mean much to you."

"Perhaps it doesn't. I can't hate you, of course."

"I know that you can't. I made it impossible for you to, because I defeated the beasts in me soon into making your acquaintance."

"No, that's not the reason."

"Then what is?"

"It's because I have been you."

I leaned forward, interested.

"What do you mean?" I asked, enthralled by what she might confess.

"I have been in your predicament. I have walked past your people and felt the same way that you felt when you looked at me. I felt you all unequal to me. And there was a time when I wished harm to you all."

When she said that, she looked away from me and went back to working on needling the dough. As she placed it in the pan to put it into the oven, I watched her.

It would be surprising to all that I was not offended. On the contrary, I was interested. Back in Hertfordshire, I enjoyed being a great study of character. And here was the greatest character study of all: two women of different creeds, pushed apart by society, grew to be friends and now are confronting the animosity that was ignited to separate them. I was fascinated, not disturbed. But I had to think of Rasby as opposed to my own perverse satisfaction.

"Does this conversation unnerve you?" I asked. "Because we can stop immediately. But if you are brave enough, I would like to know why you felt that."

"You are not angry with me?"

"No. I can't be. After all, I have said as much. Rasby, don't be afraid to open up to me. We women and men are such vicious creatures. Not everything that we have to say is meant to be pleasant. Come now, you must not say such a thing and leave me without the rest of the answer."

"It is not a pretty answer."

"True answers never are. So, confess all, and be true about it. You felt that we are unequal to you?"

"Of course, I did. A nation that is resolved to invade the rest of the world, to become an empire, taking over other species of difference, taking them, and robbing them of the best parts of their lands and then rejecting the people afterwards—or oppressing them. So, I tell myself 'at least, I am not like them'. Every once in a while, when I was being mistreated and degraded, I told myself that. I told myself that, 'at least I am not like them. I am not the villain of this story'. And it gives me a feeling of superiority."

She chuckled sadly.

"Is that not odd?" she pointed out. "We both were thinking the other unequal at the same time."

"Yes," I chuckled, "it is funny, isn't it?"

"Comical to the point of being tragic."

"Oh," I groaned, "let's not call ourselves villains, must we? No, this is the world that we were raised in, and this is the logic that we were raised on: the unfair kind."

"You were raised to find yourself superior because you are the master race," Rasby said, "and I was raised to feel superior because I wasn't like you all. What do we do when we both were victims by a doctrine that we were given from the beginning?"

I looked at a cup.

"We have a cup of tea and start from there," I answered. "Maybe that's all we can do. And maybe, that cup of tea will be enough."

"I don't want to have to *always* talk to you about the pain that my people go through," Rasby said, "just like you don't want to have to *always* talk to me about the pain that your people put us through, including others. And I don't want us to ever look at each other feeling that inequality again. I'll leave the discussion of the villain and victim relationship to when I have to shout at other people. But this is... just let me drink tea with you like this, and we will never have to speak about how to be better people, because the tea shows that we are better."

"And it's good tea."

"Yes, it is good tea."

I poured her some tea. Even though she didn't want any

more to drink, she took it anyway, drank some and went back to making bread.

Between us, Rasby and I never approached the subject again, because we didn't need to. The outside world was another matter, because it's filled with sanctimonious hypocrites who talk but never actually do what they talk about. In fact, they shade their prejudice with purity, when in reality, they never relinquished their prejudice at all. They just changed its colors so that it could camouflage better into their surroundings.

Yet with Rasby and I, we broke the primary light and saw all the many colors underneath.[1] Quite frankly, she and I didn't want to have to talk about such forms of injustice again, because we realized the simpler way was just to live and let everyone else live at the same time. Sometimes one does have to stand up and preach about such matters, because intolerance must occasionally be fought. But often, one has a tendency to go far in life if you don't walk around preaching about your principles but just adapt them and don't expect to get any awards for it. After all, equality is a given and a right, not a privilege. So, it's an implied sort of thing. I was not a superior person for overcoming my bias towards her, just like she was not a superior person for overcoming her bias towards me. You should not expect to get praised for overcoming something that you should have always been, to begin with.

That is what I am.

I am my idea of an Englishwoman, and woe betide any fool who tries to take that idea from me.

---

1. This is actually inspired by a quote that the character Saruman said in Tolkien's 'The Lord of the Rings'. But here, it's used as a tearing away of pretense and seeing the complexity of truth.

So, we drank our tea and proceeded to move along with life.

As the bread was heating up in the oven, Charlotte, Kitty, Rasby and I were in the parlor, waiting for Rasby's water to heat up, when suddenly there was a loud knock on the door.

"Who on earth..." Kitty gasped, going to the window.

"Would it be that Nicholas Higgins fellow?" Charlotte asked. "He's knocked like that before."

Kitty looked out of the window and her face lit up.

"Oh!" she cried merrily, then she yanked the front door open. "Lizzy!"

I stood up quickly, and it was just in time to see Mr. Darcy enter.

My heart filled with exhilaration at the sight of him! How much the heart realizes the loss of something when it is yanked from you, when it is severed from your side and real life separates you from the one thing that you felt such an intense link to.

So, it has been with us. And taking one look in his eye, I could see that Mr. Darcy understood me. He understood my feelings, and the very beatings of my heart.

"Lizzy!" he cried.

Rushing to each other, he grabbed me around the waist, I threw my arms around his neck, and before we knew it, our lips pressed against each other's, and we kissed passionately.

Chapter 15

Unbridled Passion

T he joys of being parted and then becoming united once again. Absence never seemed to make the heart grow fonder, in my eyes, but rather, I always feared the reverse. On the contrary, I always felt as if absence could easily make someone forgetful.

Although, with Darcy, once more my constant maxims were overturned and I saw how the waiting is both the hardest part, but also the most romantic.

The desire to see him once more had awakened the strongest parts of my emotions.

The longing to see me had clearly tugged away at his.

"I missed you," I cried, "you must not be away from me for so long again. I will forbid it!"

"I know," He insisted, "I'm sorry. I missed you as well!"

Once more, we kissed passionately and Darcy held me in his arms as we sank to the floor, each pressed against the other as if the journey that had separated us had torn our hearts and they ought to be patched up again. The ties that bind and bless them.

As we fell to the floor, myself upon his lap, I felt the

warmth and intensity of his passions as they augmented my own. The softness of his lips, the immediacy of his ardor, the cries that rang out within me that we must be bound soon, or I should go mad.

I would have him for my life, for my love, and within my very soul. And to think, that I had almost tore myself away from such an embrace, from such a true attachment, for the sake of a prejudice that was never worth upholding, for deceptions that should have never been thrust upon me. To have once willfully misunderstand the truest man in one's life, to know that such greatness almost slipped from your grasp, would fill one with regrets. All regrets now had been laid flat, had been fully eradicated, and peace, passion, and pleasure took its place.

Now, I felt alive.

Now, for so long, I felt as if the whole world was sweeping out before my very feet, and all was giving way to a swift sunrise of hope and belief. Of love.

After a few seconds, we eventually found the self-control to release one another, but only because of the prickling upon my neck, of the sensing that we were being watched.

"Wait for a moment," I whispered to Darcy.

"Must I—"

"My sisters and friends, Mr. Darcy."

"Oh."

We all turned and Kitty, Charlotte, Margaret Hale, and Rasby were staring at us.

"Rasby," Kitty said, "sorry, but you can't take a bath just yet."

"Yes, I can see that," Rasby said, "besides, I've been thinking that maybe we ought to go and pay a visit to Nicholas and Mary. They might wish to see us."

"What a splendid idea."

"I'll remove the water," Charlotte responded, going to the fireplace, and removing the pots of boiling water from over the flames.

All three women filed out of the house. Kitty, being the last to do so, looked down at the floor as she held the door slightly ajar, while not looking at us.

"I understand the impulse that you both are undergoing. I see the passion. While I know that you both are prudent, I can only give you both an hour. No more and no less. Do the best you can to try and restrain, but if you can't...we will understand. An hour, mind you."

With that, she closed the door, and Darcy and I were alone.

When I looked into his eyes, I saw the depth of Darcy's joy, and I also glimpsed my reflection in them.

"You are beautiful," I whispered.

"Am I?" he asked.

"Yes, you are. Have I never said that before?"

"Whether you have or not, never fear saying it again. Never fear my love for knowing that you found something about me worth loving."

"And I will never forget it. I only can't forgive myself for not having seen it sooner."

"I was a fool. I didn't help you. I shall spend my life making you see the better sides of myself now."

He kissed me passionately once more.

"An hour is all that we have," he whispered savagely. "Enough talking. Enough talking for now."

Closing the space between us, he pressed his lips against mine. Instinctively, I ran my fingers through his hair, and it seemed to unleash his passion even further. He cradled me in his lap, and his lips ran along my cheek and down to the creases of my neck.

So small a touch, such a simple thing and it felt as if it was all the world.

"One hour!" he whispered harshly, "one bloody hour!"

Standing me up, he took my hand and pulled me along to the steps.

"Come on," he insisted.

"Darcy, we cannot..."

He placed his foot on the first step, but froze when he heard me say those words. There was disappointment etched across his face. More than disappointment, in fact. Rather, it looked as if I had slapped him across the cheek. What I would have given to have his happiness returned to him.

Turning back to me, Darcy's face now bore pain. Sadness. Pain from a happy moment being torn from him. Loss of two becoming one.

I held his hand.

"I just... I want our wedding night to be special," I insisted.

"Whatever happens today, it will be. I just... I don't know when we will marry, and I cannot bear it any longer. I'm dying inside, Elizabeth."

"So am I...we can take our time."

I kissed his hand.

"Come then," I agreed with him, "I will go with you to the ends of the world. And to our bed."

Once more, he kissed me and then rushed up the steps, hastened into my bedroom and then we kissed once more.

After our lips separated, he rested his face against my own, our noses touching, and he stared deeply into my eyes.

"Is Charlotte willing to take your place?" he asked.

"She still does not know," I answered.

"Will Maria take Jane's place?"

"She still does not know either. I'm sorry that I do not give you better news."

"I come with good news enough for the both of us."

"You do?" I asked eagerly, "Lady Catherine approves of our marriage? Honestly, I wouldn't care if she did or didn't, but it would be a joy nevertheless if she did."

"It took a while, but she has accepted it."

"She forgives me for not being Anne?"

"We'll speak of this later. Not now. Let us love each other and that be the end of it."

Turning me around, he began to unfasten my skirt as I removed my blouse. I made quick work of my corset, unfastening it as quickly as I could before I halted.

He felt my hesitancy.

"Elizabeth," he said, standing behind me, "you stop."

"Yes, I do."

He placed his hands on my shoulders, while I still only wore my shift and undergarment.

"Are you afraid of me now?" he asked. "Of this?"

"No," I responded, feeling utterly overpowered by my own logical defense of what I was about to do. I didn't understand my own mode and manner...how was I accepting this? All that I had been taught, believed, and felt, was now being thrown to the wayside. "That is what scares me."

"I am here, nor am I going anywhere."

"I suppose that's why I am not ashamed of what we are about to do. I know that you are here, that you always will be, and that you will not forsake me. I know that you are a good man, and so it justifies this erroneous deed."

"Erroneous?"

"Darcy, a kiss or two between both sexes is something that can occur, but we are taught that is wrong. We are not man and wife yet, and this is everything that I have been trained to be against. But why now? Why am I willing to abandon all those principles so eagerly? Why am I not afraid? Why do I not care?"

I looked over my shoulder and into his eyes.

"Are you marrying a wicked woman, I wonder?" I asked him, still not ashamed.

"No, you are not. For I would be a wicked man if I were to judge you for something that I am."

"Men are allowed to be that way."

"And so you ought to be as well."

Running his hands along my neck, I sighed, feeling the softness of his gentle caress.

"Your wickedness is wonderful, and it is also wise. You chose me, and I am not turning away. I will never turn away for a moment. Let my constancy assure you that we are one, even if not tied by a ceremony. Here and now, we are one."

Once more, he leaned downward and pressed his lips against mine as he raised up my shift and then pulled it over my head.

Afterwards, I undid my other undergarments as he removed his jacket, waistcoat, cravat, and breeches. The only thing that remained was his shirt, because he lacked the time to remove it when he saw me bare in front of him.

He still stood behind me and looked down at the curves of my back.

"Don't worry," he assured me, "I will be gentle until we are both ready."

Slowly he moved his hands from the back of my neck and ran his fingertips slowly down my shoulders. Afterwards, he moved them along my back and slowly, he massaged the back of my hips.

With equal care, he moved his hands downward, and he

placed his fingers along my bottom and began to run his hands all over it.

I cried out, leaning forward, and grabbing the edge of the bed, to steady myself.

"Do I hurt you?" he asked, slowing down.

"No!" I cried desperately, "do not even think of stopping. Please, you make me happy now."

"I will not. I want you to enjoy this. I want you to love this act and not see the wickedness of it. Don't be afraid to cry out, Lizzy. I want to know that I am making you happy."

He continued to run his hands all over my bottom, then my thighs, and each touch felt like it was a walk amongst the clouds in the heavens.

At last, he pulled me up and he held me against his person. My back was pressed against his front as he wrapped his arms around my waist, I twisted my neck to see into his eyes and he kissed me once more.

Our kisses did not end as he ran his hands down my chest, cupped my breasts within his hands and his touch became more urgent. I moaned out into Darcy's mouth, for his lips were still pressed against mine. Rather than release the kiss, it seemed to excite him as he deepened the embrace. Even more desperately, his hands moved all over my breasts, as if he was clinging to them like we would never be parted.

Every touch, I invited.

Every ministration, I desired.

I feared this was the end of his affections before I would no longer become a maid, however, that was not to be so. When he finished paying all attention to the top half of my body, I felt his fingers slowly slide down my stomach, each touch was like that of a tingle, he pressed one hand in between my thighs and began to press his fingers within me deeply.

Once more, I moaned out in his mouth, and my cries were stifled by the kiss that would forever linger.

My loud proclamations did not decrease Darcy's passions but only swelled his pride and satisfaction. It was the ultimate encouragement.

Rather than decrease his attentions, he thrust his fingers deeper within me and more briskly. I cried out, with only his lips to stifle my pleasure, then Darcy placed the other hand on my breast again and began to massage me briskly on both parts of my person.

Was this love?

If so, there was no wickedness to it, nothing ugly or vain. It was perfection; it was bliss. It was the ultimate form of our bond.

"I make you happy," he said, while his lips were still pressed against mine.

"Yes. Do not stop. Please! Let us stay here forever. We must never leave this bedroom again."

"The bedrooms at Pemberley shall be more sufficient for our purpose. You shall love them, Lizzy. You shall be its mistress. I will always be your husband, from this day forth."

He thrust his fingers deeper within me, and I cried out as I keeled over.

"Try to remain quiet, dearest," he insisted, "I pride myself in making you moan, but I don't want you to be talked of. Cover your mouth if you need to because I am not done. What I would give to remain here forever. Now, brace yourself, Lizzy. I am far from done pleasing you."

He kept his one hand in between my thighs. Next, he lowered his other hand from my breast and placed it on my bottom once more. Then he pressed his hand deep within it and began to press his fingers deeper, between my thighs, from both directions.

I keeled over, grabbing the covers on my bed, pressed them against my mouth to stifle my moans.

There was a little pain involved, but the pain was what I enjoyed about it. He ran his hands over and around inside of me, and words could not be described.

He continued in this way for an eternity that I still felt was all too brief.

"Please," I gasped, "do not stop."

"I will not," he insisted, "because you are right. I shall give us something to look forward to. I will not take you in full till our wedding night." I felt his lips kiss my back. "You will be a maid when we wed, for your own peace of mind. I will have you regret nothing. But I will give you this, my love. I will give you all of this."

He laid me on the bed and still continued to rub his hands deeper within me. More and more, I had to press my mouth against the bed, to quiet my cries of exhilaration.

This continued till I felt my body spasm, waves of ecstasy shot through me, my nerves peaked, and I collapsed on the bed, unable to move.

When I rolled over, I looked at Darcy. Having lost all ability to move for a moment, I must have looked a fright, but Darcy only looked down at me, his eyes twinkling.

"You are beautiful."

"And you, sir, are a marvel of a man."

"And you are my lady."

He laid down on top of me and I wrapped my arms around him. For some reason, I felt like being protective. I felt as if, if I held him there, and never let him leave the room, I would be shielding him from the smoke and gray of the outside world, of the conflict that rose and fell whenever we humans interact and clash with each other, and of the chaos that it could ensue.

"I do hope Charlotte takes the post," he stressed, holding his arms tightly against me.

"So do I," I said, "if so, we could do this all the time."

"You liked it?" he chuckled.

"Were my moans not enough? You were right. As long as a woman finds a man who she can trust, who she can depend upon, there is nothing wicked about this. I trust you."

"And I will never give you reason not to."

"But even the act itself—I am wondering now that maybe there is nothing wicked about it, in general. We are taught to fear the act of fornication, of it being quite the sin, of purity of manner. But surely, an act that brings such self-satisfaction and emotional completion, cannot be evil."

"It is not, Lizzy. It never was. I appreciate the purity of things, but we humans have the inclination to take it too far. Sometimes, I wonder if it is all down to a sense of control."

"People using shame in the act of carnal embrace to control each other?"

"Yes."

"Perhaps so," I acknowledged, "after all, we humans do often have the obsession with controlling each other's lives. I suppose it's in our nature, despite repercussions of when it appeals to our more frightening sides. Oh dear!"

"What?"

"Here we are, just having made the ultimate form of love, and we are being philosophical? What is the matter with us?"

"We are a strange pair, aren't we?"

"Yes, we are. We ought to be talking of love, but that's not what we are doing. Oh well, perhaps it's for the best, because speaking of control, I still am surprised that Lady Catherine would approve of me. Between losing a child—truly, losing a child must be the worst thing for a mother—to me not being the ideal choice for you, I still wonder that she said yes."

"Well," Darcy sighed, "I am not going to deny that it did do a great deal of bargaining to achieve that."

I raised an eyebrow and looked down at him.

"Bargaining? Darcy, did you sell your soul?"

"No, not so much that as...Lizzy, we cannot marry in Milton."

"What do you mean? Many of our friends are here." I read his mind. "Oh! Darcy, is Lady Catherine ordering us to marry at Hunsford Church, on her estate?"

Darcy looked at me sheepishly.

"Before you get a little disgruntled at the idea, Elizabeth, I need you to do this, not only for me, but also for my aunt. Whatever her faults, I do love her. She's my aunt. Also, think of it from her perspective. She lost a child."

"Her only child."

"Precisely. The idea of arranging a triple wedding is the precise arrangement that she needs to help her recover. She needs to feel as if there is family beside her now. I fear her being alone. Also, to have the county see us all wed, and her arrange dinner parties will give her that spark."

"Oh, I had not thought of that. I was being selfish."

"No, you weren't. Despite all initial inclinations we had when coming to the North, this did become our home for so long that we assumed it best to marry here."

"The Thorntons, Higginses and Bouchers won't be there to see us wed. Nor will the Pitchers. And unless we can convince them to come, the Hales might not be there either. But I can see that Lady Catherine's recovery is important. In fact, it might be a slight for us not to do it."

"Yes, precisely. And there's more to it. She wants to arrange everything."

"Well, as long as I get a say in what my wedding gown looks like, I think I can oblige."

I chuckled.

"Yes, I had an inkling. I will write to her about that. I'm sure my aunt would agree."

"Well, I must tell Jane and Kitty, but they will be amenable to the idea. They just want to get married, and the arrangements would not be as significant to them. I am sure your aunt will be satisfied. She must miss Colonel Fitzwilliam as well."

"She does," Darcy said, smiling.

"What is that smile for?"

"Because she will have little cause to miss him again. After all, he will be with her very often from now on."

"How so?"

"Because...she is making him the heir of Rosings Park."

When hearing that, I felt as if I could be knocked down with a feather—thank goodness I was already laying down.

"Colonel Fitzwilliam is to be her heir?" I gasped.

"Yes."

I laughed.

"Oh, my goodness. It makes all the sense in the world, now that I come to think of it. Rosings Park could not have a better heir to take it over than the Colonel. After all, Lady Catherine adores him."

"Yes, she does."

"And if Kitty and he marry, then my sister...will be the eventual mistress of Rosings Park?"

"Yes, Kitty will. We must not tell her until she and Colonel Fitzwilliam are together. But yes, your sister and my cousin will not only inherit the estate, but also the title. They will become Sir and Lady Fitzwilliam."

I sighed, so amazed that I could not believe our family's fortune, after so much misfortune.

"Unbelievable!" I cried.

"It is fascinating, I know."

"Not just that, but the irony of it all. Here, in Milton, we fell to the very lowest in life, and only for the catastrophe to overturn on itself and find the greatest happiness of all. It is almost too good to be true—but true it is. And I am glad of it. Jane, Kitty, and I...and oh! We can save Mary as well. Then again, I am not so certain. From all her letters, Mary seems to love working."

"Yes. I think that she wouldn't want us to tear her from her right to toil and labor."

"For some, that gives them purpose in life. Mary has her purpose now; heaven forbid I take that from her. And Lydia!" I laughed. "Three rich sisters married to men of great estates and extensive grounds. She will be forever visiting."

"Yes, she might. Well, I like Denny, therefore, I think I can endure it."

"Thank you for that. She is growing to be something better than when she was back home. Or maybe she is growing up and was given the time to. We shall see."

I looked down at him. His eyes smiled while I laughed.

"Can one die of happiness?" I asked, marveled at it all. "After all the adventures and misadventures that we all endured, and only for us all to arrive at the perfect natural conclusions."

"Yes. Against all my mistakes of bad advice to Bingley, toward myself, and it all found itself working out in the happiest of ways. Truly, I wonder if we humans sometimes make things worse by making plans."

"Who knows, eh?"

"Yes, who knows? Whoever knows?"

Suddenly, we heard the front door open downstairs.

Berserker!

Darcy and I transformed from two people in fond embrace to two mice scurrying around, trying to find our clothing.

"That was an hour?" I hissed as we frantically shifted about.

"I don't think so," Darcy whispered, terrified.

"Hello?" Jane's voice cried. "Anyone home? Maria and I have returned."

I closed my eyes.

It wasn't Kitty, Margaret Hale and Rasby.

Jane and Maria had returned sooner than expected.

Darcy and I had been caught red-handed.

Chapter 16

Good News

" I 'm here, Jane and Maria," I called down to them. "I was resting. Give me a few minutes to make myself presentable, and then I will be down momentarily."

There was a momentary pause.

"Very well," I heard Jane say. "Where is Kitty?"

"She went to visit the Higginses. Charlotte, Margaret and Rasby are with her."

"Do they know you are here?"

"Yes," I said, warily. I didn't know why, but there was something in Jane's voice that hinted at her being dubious about something.

"Maria," I heard Jane say, "can you do me a favor and go to the Higginses so that Charlotte knows you are here? Also, could you tell Nicholas that we have some food for the Bouchers if they need our assistance?"

"Very well," Maria said, as innocent as she wished and then she was off. When I heard the door close, Darcy and I looked at each other. For some reason or the other, we both knew. Looking into each other's eyes, we just knew.

Suddenly, we heard Jane's footsteps approach the stairs.

"Lizzy," Jane said, "are you well?"

"Yes, I am."

"Is Mr. Darcy well also?"

I bit my lip. Jane knew he was here. Taking one look at him, we both flinched. It felt as if our parents were downstairs, and we were children who were guilty of breaking a rule.

"Mr. Darcy," Jane called, "be honest, how was your journey to Kent? There's no point in ignoring me."

Darcy gave me a pleading look. All I could do was nod and give him a 'oh well, might as well own to our situation' look.

"It was very well, thank you," Darcy replied.

"I think it's time you both came down, don't you think?" Jane said. "You both really don't have much time before anyone else returns."

"We are coming," I said, filled with anxiety on the matter.

"I know."

Darcy and I turned back to each other.

"Why do I feel as if we are in deep trouble?" Darcy asked me as he helped me get dressed.

"Because we are. My mother's not here, so an older sister is equally as good at bringing on the shame."

"Too true. I am scared, Lizzy."

"So am I. Scared of Jane, eh? Now this is a new experience."

We dressed and went downstairs. Our movements were slow, for we felt as if we were about to face the Angel of Death.

And there Jane was. We found her sitting down, her hands folded on the table.

"Jane," I began.

"Yes, Lizzy?"

Her calmness was the most unsettling thing to witness. Darcy and I stood there, facing her with such intense dread. If only she would scream at us. That would have been easier. But no, she chose silence. And that was the most painful punishment of all.

Jane looked at Mr. Darcy. She was as still as a statue.

"Good day, Mr. Darcy. I am happy that you are well."

"Yes," was all that he could say. "Thank you."

Even his familiar scowl was gone! In its place was the face of a little boy who wanted to run away and hide.

Jane reached behind her, picked up a satchel bag and placed it on the table. It belonged to Mr. Darcy.

"It was in the corner," Jane said, "thrown aside. I had the suspicion that you wouldn't have left it behind."

"No," Darcy admitted. "I would not have. Miss Bennet, lord knows what you think of me right now."

"With all due respect, Mr. Darcy," Jane said simply and serenely, "but you don't know what I think about you now. I think it would hurt you to find out what that is."

Darcy was silenced by this.

"Your sister and I will get married," he stressed.

"I am still a maid, Jane," I added.

"Yes. She is."

"Do you swear to that?" Jane asked, still so simply that she might as well have been an ice demon. Every word she uttered sent chills down my spine.

"Yes, I do."

"Jane," I began, "it is partly my fault."

"I don't need to hear any more," Jane said flatly. She

leaned forward. "This moment shall be kept between us. Are we agreed?"

"Yes," I rushed out, "very much so."

"Entirely," Darcy confirmed.

"And this moment will also be in the past, and not the present. Until you are wed, you will never do this again. Are we agreed?"

"Yes," Darcy and I said, in unison.

"Good," Jane replied, "I am happy we agree. And I shall be watching you closely from now on. You both are very much in love, and love makes it hard to always control oneself. Therefore, you are excused this once."

"Thank you," was all that I could manage.

"Now," Jane said, "how is Lady Catherine, Mr. Darcy? My condolences on such a tragic loss."

"She is maintaining. But she has a request to make of you."

"A request?"

"More of an order, really," I corrected. Darcy gave me a look. "What? It is true."

"An order?" Jane repeated.

"My aunt has suffered a great loss. She requests that you, Kitty and Lizzy have a triple wedding at Hunsford and be married at Rosings Park."

"Oh," Jane said, "Well, that is a relief. As much as I would prefer to marry here in Milton, I understand why your aunt wants us in her life right now. She needs this. I can speak for Bingley. I am sure that he will be amenable to the idea."

"Yes, Bingley would be," Darcy confirmed.

"Now, we ought to go to the Higginses and tell Kitty the news."

Darcy and I agreed to this, and we opened the door just

as Plato was about to knock on it. Truly, we opened the door to him as his fist was in the air and he was about to tap against the wood of the door. It was quite a comical sight.

"Did we really just find you about to knock on the door just as we opened it?" I asked him.

"Yes," he said, both amazed and perplexed, "I suppose you did." He lowered his hand. "I came as a herald of invitation."

"Oh, how lovely," Jane said, "what invitation is it?"

"I came to inform you that the regiment will be holding a dinner, to honor its last day being in Milton. I issued an invitation for you all to attend. It will take place on Wednesday evening. If you are not otherwise engaged."

"We should all be able to," I said, "but come with us to the Higginses. Your sister is there with the Lucases, and Miss Hale. You can sit with us for a while and then issue the invitation when we return."

"Very well. Lead the way, Miss Bennet," Plato said, taking her arm. We followed Jane and Plato down the street.

"How was your time with the Kirkpatricks?" I asked Jane. "Did Maria like Little Molly, and the Kirkpatrick children?"

Jane sighed happily.

"She did, fortunately. They were on their very best behavior, and Mr. and Mrs. Kirkpatrick liked her as well."

"But did Maria varnish you with the impression that she was willing to consider taking your place?" I asked.

"I did not ask her. I figured that it would be better to not influence her at all. I shall just have to wait, and hopefully, I shall be rewarded for it."

"If so," Plato said, "the South will take you away from this place. I shall miss looking upon you all. You were quite the charming set."

"Plato, you flatter us."

"Flattery is a soldier's trade; one must always brush up on it."

When we arrived at the Higgins's home, we were all packed in like sausages.

"Mr. Darcy," Margaret said, when seeing me enter with his arm linked in mine. "You are safely returned."

"Yes, I have," Darcy replied, "healthy and whole."

"How is your aunt?" Margaret asked.

"She is doing her best to recover. Thank you. But I suppose that there may never be sufficient time for her to recover from it. Forgive me if I speak in tragic tones."

"Losing a child is not to be easily forgotten," Nicholas Higgins confirmed. "Yer don' offend me for bringin' it up."

"Yes, well... you both are grieving parents, aren't you?"

"Yer aunt may be a fancy lady, but when it comes to losin' a child, we all become quite the same."

We all looked in the corner to where Bessy used to sit. It was so strange. She was not there, and yet, it felt like she was, all the same.

"They never fully leave us," Nicholas commented. Nicholas wasn't upset for seeing us, but rather merely was a little self-conscious by having a man like Mr. Darcy in his home. Either way, between losing Bessy, I suppose he had grown accustomed to our faces.

Deciding that it would be best to change the subject, Nicholas turned to the Lucas sisters. "Are yer enjoyin' yer time here in Milton?"

"We are," Maria answered. "Of course, it is different than anything else that we are accustomed to. However, once we begin to live here, we feel that we will soon grow accustomed to Milton ways."

When hearing this, I felt a whirlwind of revelations rise within me. Sharply, I turned to Darcy.

He, too, felt the change of the winds in the room.

Lastly, I turned to Jane. Her countenance went from serene to hopeful agitation.

Did we all hear correctly?

Then I looked at Kitty, and she looked equally as hopeful to me.

Next, we turned to Margaret, who also looked at Maria with wonder.

"Live here?" Jane repeated. "Maria and Charlotte, is this true?"

Maria looked at Charlotte.

"Oh," Maria commented, "I thought it was understood."

"I never got around to telling them the news," Charlotte said. Turning, she looked at us.

"Last night, Maria and I came to a decision. We just were waiting to make sure that we had committed to the right path. We both have agreed to take your places here, in Milton, Jane and Lizzy. I will accept the notetaking post. And Maria will become the Kirkpatricks' governess."

It couldn't be! Fortune could not find itself out so easily. But could it?

"Is this true?" Jane asked, standing up in awe. "You really mean it?"

"We mean it," Maria said, "we assure you. We shall take your place. Now you can marry. And we are happy for you."

Could it be? It was too good to be true. The happiest moment of my life had finally arrived. And all was thanks to the Lucas sisters, who had held steadfast to me.

And I believed it—better than reportingly!

I smiled.

I laughed.

We all did. Expecting Darcy and I to be the happiest couple in the world.

Nothing could go wrong now!

Life had finally taken us out of the darkness and into the light.

We were to be married.

Our paths were free, and we could live, love, and prosper. All was right at this time.

After all, nothing bad could happen now, surely.

It turned out... I couldn't have been more wrong.

End of Book IV[1]

---

1. There is an Afterword on the next page, in case the reader wants to understand the choices that I made in the novel.

Afterword

Hello, Reader, sorry for the delay in publication. But I'm a working-class little snip, and these last couple of months, I've had to cover more shifts, because I have a simple dream: one day I will afford to have health insurance. But slowly and surely, I'm getting closer to affording it. Fingers crossed.

Therefore, I've been working seven days a week for the last month. Literally, I had to bring my laptop on the bus with me every day so that I could write going *to* and *from* work. That's where this book was written: on public transit. Quite frankly, I'm lucky that I haven't gotten robbed yet, with how I flagrantly parade my technology on my lap every day. Thank goodness for small miracles!

If a publication of mine ever comes out later than expected, it's not me being lazy, I assure you. I simply work a lot, for survival. I wish that I could release books at the time that you deserve, but my time is often not my own. But I will always focus on getting my books complete as fast as I can. Cross my heart.

Now, onto pressing matters that are more interesting: the contents of this book.

Yes, Reader, I did something shocking: I had Anne de Bourgh die.

I wish for you to know that I mean no ill will toward Anne de Bourgh. I never really hated her because, most of the time, I felt bad that her sickly constitution held her back so much, while her mother's dominating presence made it impossible for Anne to bloom in the way that she might have. Lady Catherine loves her daughter, of that we are certain. In that way, she and Mrs. Bennet are very similar.

Mrs. Bennet and Lady Catherine are:

- Characters of mean understanding.
- Dominating presences
- Excessive pride
- Believing themselves to always be right
- Both tried to force their child to marry someone that they do not love—and that chosen person is their child's cousin.
- Are often pressing their will on others.
- But also care for their families and children immensely.

The chief difference is that Mrs. Bennet was not born to a prestigious position, while Lady Catherine was born and maintained her wealth. The world's chief difference for them indicates how people's perspective can change on a person when one has money, and the other doesn't. Due to her wealth, Lady Catherine's personality is respected, whereas with Mrs. Bennet, she has no wealth to shield herself from other's observing her behavior.

Another difference is that, while both women love company, Mrs. Bennet does like it when others speak, whereas Lady Catherine talks in a way where it's dictatorial;

she seldom needs a response. She likes people to talk at, rather than to talk with. That being said, perhaps Mrs. Bennet could have turned that way, if she had the wealth to allow her to be so. We will never know.

Now, back to Anne de Bourgh. The sole reason that I began to contemplate her departure from the story was merely out of a desire to be creative on Lady Catherine's part.

I have written Anne as the sickly and silent creature that she is. I've written her where she stands up to her mother and grows more independent. And other times I've had her become rambunctious and choose the man that she loves, against all odds. Never before had I had her undergo a tragedy, which was wholly new for me.

However, it led me down different avenues, because this is the first time that I get to write Lady Catherine as a grieving mother. This allowed me to take Lady Catherine, a character who I usually just keep as an antagonizing force, turn her upside down and make a creature worth pitying. After all, she loved her daughter. Even though she could be overbearing, it was all out of love and wanting the best for Anne. And the worst nightmare that could happen to a caring parent is for their child to die before them. From what I've observed, if that happens, a parent feels as if they have been galvanized, and are constantly dying within. By that occurring, it offered many possibilities of what roads the story could walk down and give the reader something I hadn't given them before. It makes Lady Catherine feel more humanized. Hopefully, you won't think it was vicious. It just allowed me to do something different.

Here's the joyous idea of it: when I first had the idea of Lady Catherine losing Anne, it didn't occur to me, till a while afterwards, that it would conveniently lead to Colonel

Fitzwilliam now having the fortune to marry Kitty, the one woman he adored. It was one of those happy accidents that came out of the narrative.

And ultimately, it worked out, because Lady Catherine gets an heir to a nephew that she loves and loves her. Her affection for him is displayed in how she speaks of him. Now, of course, it could be assumed that she exaggerates his love for her, but I do not believe so. Hear me out before you laugh and say that I am wrong (which the reader has every right to do so). First, Colonel Fitzwilliam is a genuinely easy-going person with a comfortable air about him. He is not the sort to be disobliging to a relative of his who prefers him. Second, even though he never praises his aunt, Lady Catherine doesn't strike me as the sort of woman who would be so much attached to a relative if he didn't show her any affection.

I know that Lady Catherine gives off the impression of being a woman who doesn't always see reality for what it is but rather watches it through a perception filter—as all of us humans do from time to time. Though she may do it to excess, I actually believe Lady Catherine is capable of seeing a situation for what it is. The reason I think this is because of when she goes all the way to Longbourn just to order Elizabeth Bennet to never engage herself to Mr. Darcy, I think it's because she is secretly aware of the reality of the situation. For, if she thoroughly believed that Mr. Darcy wanted to marry her daughter, she would never have felt the need to go to Hertfordshire. She would feel secure in knowing that Mr. Darcy was attached to Anne. That *would* be her being completely out of touch with reality.

But no! She decides to leave her elegant home and make her way into the Hertfordshire countryside to order a woman to not marry her nephew.

Also, why didn't she just go to Darcy and request him not to marry Elizabeth? After all, he's her nephew. That could only happen if she was very aware that she had no overall influence on Darcy. For after all, if Darcy wanted to marry Anne, he would have done it already. So, she travels to Longbourn to appeal to what she would have assumed would be the weaker side of the equation. She assumes that Elizabeth Bennet would shirk under her influence and be easily guilted into abandoning any desire to marry Darcy. She was dead wrong. But that is the actions of a woman who is fully aware of the situation. She knows that Darcy doesn't want to choose Anne, so she goes to the woman who he might choose and tries to frighten her off. It's vicious, selfish, and wrong, but it's self-aware.

Thus, because I feel like Lady Catherine's actions is committed by a woman who truthfully knows what's going on, I don't think she would see affection in a relative, if there was none. Thus, when she feels that Colonel Fitzwilliam does love her, it's probably very true. For, despite her dictatorial habits of always wishing to control everything, she ultimately can see when affection is real versus when it's not there at all. Therefore, when Colonel Fitzwilliam becomes her heir, it is perhaps the only thing that could help Lady Catherine recover. She loses the daughter that she loved but gets compensated by her gaining a beloved nephew as her future.

I hope that this explains why I was sacrilegious and killed off one of Jane Austen's characters. As strange as it is to admit, it was actually done out of love.

Now onto the other part of the tale that could raise some opinions amongst the audience: the discussion Lizzy and Rasby had when it came to racism. Readers, I understand when such discussions are unwanted to read about in stories like these. After all, who wants their daily dose of discussion on inequality in a series where you read to escape? Also, how dare I have Elizabeth Bennet, the ultimate heroine, acknowledge some racial prejudice inside herself. I know that this sort of writing can turn readers away.

First, this was not done out of any reason of suffering under the infliction of white guilt. It was done, because honestly, I thought it made Elizabeth more interesting. I began to write Elizabeth in a way where she is beginning to become very perfect. And she has a right to be. Yet, another great aspect about Elizabeth's character is that she is *not* perfect. She owns up to this herself. That's why readers can identify with her. She is the full growth process of the female and male mind:

- An assumption of feeling superior.
- Then to have the proverbial rug swept out from under your feet and you discover just how imperfect you are.
- And the humility that follows after we have fallen.

It's a tale as old as time. Well, I have reached the point in my narrative where I have made Elizabeth into a woman who I feel is almost ideal. I don't know what the reader's opinion of my take on her is, but she just feels like I pour the better sides of humanity into. And I'm going to do that for the remainder of the series. But here's the thing: that's not Elizabeth. She is a very idealistic creature in some ways, but she needs a flaw every now and again to give the reader the chance to identify with her.

So, I gave her that sort of prejudice, but I also gave it to her for her not to be ashamed of. Elizabeth is basically saying, 'Yes, I come from a culture that did that horrible thing to yours and I can't erase it. But quite frankly, I'm not in the mood to walk the halls weeping over my own guilt. That's not productive to either of us. What I will do...is just confront it, and never forget all that happened between us. And then we can progress from there.' That's Elizabeth's mentality. She knows the errors of her nation's/race's history, but she can't undo it. So, this is her admitting that she's as flawed as the rest of us, but she's not going to let it hold her down. No. She will live, love, and prosper.

This scene was done, firstly, because it honestly came out organically. You know how when you begin writing, your instincts take over and you write things that just flow naturally. You don't even think first. No. You trust your instincts and come what may. That's what happened here.

Secondly, I kept it in there, because again, it showed Lizzy as flawed.

Thirdly, it's because Elizabeth is us. In Jane's Austen's timeless genius, every heroine she has written is another part of US all. Even some of her lesser characters are us. Elizabeth's appeal is that she is us, through and through. And we all are human. And we all, against our will, notice difference. What I mean is that, sometimes, our prejudices are our fault. Other times, it's not. We all are born into a world where we are literally trained to see difference and fear it. We are all born with the capacity to treat others equally, but the world won't let us. We have to be reminded of our differences on a daily basis. Now, this is all well and good, if we were taught the basic principles that difference is still equal. But that's not the message we were given since infancy. There is a unique and tragic melding, when it comes to life: where all that is the same works, and all that is different, isn't. From physical appearance to basic opinions. You can't think differently than the person next to you. You can't have different customs. Because 'same' is the Age Of The Thing. Even when we are attempting diversity, it can be done in the strangest of routes. We change genders of a character or change their race. This can work sometimes, (in fact, it should always work in theatre/classics adapted to the screen in modern ways) but other times it shows how the only way that you can achieve diversity is *not* by creating new diverse characters, but changing the race/gender of preexisting characters...and thus making them the *same* as the people who you are trying to appeal to. By definition, we are now saying that a person of color cannot identify with a white character, or a white person cannot identify with a character of color. Or a character has to change from a male to a female, because that's the way a female can identify with them...but we all know that we women have the strong ability to NOT be so shallow. We can identify with men in the same way that they can identify with us. To be able to identify with difference and treat it with the same equality as you would treat those who are the same as you is the true achievement. Therefore, sometimes, to change a gender/race of an established character (unless you are doing modernizations/theatre) can sometimes pose two outcomes. One is good and the other is bad:

1. It's good because you are reaching a plateau where you can feel comfortable putting any race in any situation. Or...
2. You make the mistake of actually preaching the message of 'you can only identify with a character if you make them the same as you', rather than accepting that they are different and connecting with them all the same.

Long story short, it's a slippery slope. This has always been difficult for me because I was raised in a time where we loved the difference of things.

When growing up, I saw movies like 'The Pagemaster', where you had the incredible talent of people like Christopher Lloyd, but there was another thing I loved where you had African American actress Whoopi Goldberg and British Caucasian actor Sir Patrick Stewart acting against each other. Then they acted together again in Star Trek. What I loved about that was that I got to see two entirely different individuals act together and be on the same level with each other. They were both different races, genders and from different nations. That was the beauty of it. But to remove Sir Patrick Stewart from the equation would have been a crime to me, not because he is a white male, but because the difference between him and Whoopi was the point.

This continued with all of my experience with Star Trek, from the original series to the modern ones. The blending of Caucasian actors/directors/writers with non-Caucasian actors/directors/writers, as well as American and non-American people working on it, was the epitome of beauty.

The same went for when I watched 'Maid in Manhattan' with Ralph Fiennes and Jennifer Lopez. Once more, two different genders, races, and nations. Then there was 'Kiss the Girls' with Morgan Freeman and Ashley Judd. In the movie 'Unleashed', you had Jet Li, Morgan Freeman, and Kerry Condon. Once again, *three* different races and genders. Then, from a national standpoint, there was the movie 'The Golden Compass', where you literally had all these very talented British and Australian actors in it... and Sam Elliot in all his American glory. From a writing standpoint, you have writers like the British genius, Neil Gaiman, who has projects where both British and Americans work together. To me, that is glorious.

Therefore, to remove anyone from the equation of the image doesn't work. So, it's very difficult, in the world we are in, to praise the world's achievements of 'equality' and inclusion', when those same people always seem to be excluding someone or other. How do you function in a world where there is exclusion on both sides?

Well, first, that was where Elizabeth Bennet comes in. She's white, and she doesn't have to hate herself for it. Just like Rasby is black, and she doesn't have to hate herself for it, no matter if her inclusion in this story makes some in the audience uncomfortable, just by her mere presence.

And that brings us back to Rasby and Plato. I don't want to believe that their presence in the novel affects anyone's enjoyment of it. I believe my readers come to the story, for the sake of the story, and you take these characters for what they are. When it comes to their involvement in the tale, if the reader is awaiting some grand moment in the narrative to explain their presence in the story, I should let you know... that moment is never coming.

Raspberry and Plato are in the tale simply to exist and be a part of the story, for two reasons. First, they are there just to do what all of us wish to do in this world: simply live and be allowed to live. But it's not just that. The second reason they are there is not just because of the effect that they have on Miss Austen's and Miss Gaskell's central characters, but the effect that those central characters have on them.

With Lizzy, Margaret, Kitty, Darcy, Thornton, and everyone else, they represent something: the plethora of Caucasian individuals who live among people of color and that's it. They neither walk around supporting racial discrimination, nor do they walk around giving racial harmony speeches. They choose to do the latter with their actions, just let them live and let live. They don't walk around preaching about racial justice, because they do it just by accepting people like Rasby and Plato in their lives and thinking no lesser of them. Those sorts of people are those that never get awards in life, but they are the most tolerant people. They see difference for a few minutes, and then they don't care to notice it anymore. To notice and then not notice. That is the challenge, and the journey. Of course, there are times where you must speak up about injustice because an oppression is occurring. But from a day to day basis, just letting equality be a silent 'given', works wonders.

All the characters in this novel are a remembrance to the many Caucasians, historically, who noticed difference for five seconds, and then stopped noticing ten seconds later. And as a result, they were willing to live, and let others around them live, without any need to defend or offend, because they already accepted. Those are the ones who will NEVER get into any history books, but they were there the whole time, quietly accepting and subtly doing the right thing. That is why Raspberry and Plato are in this book. They are there to celebrate those who just live and are willing to let everyone else live on the same plane as them. But the only way for Elizabeth, Darcy, Kitty, Margaret, Thornton, etc. are able to do that, is by having the Pitchers in the tale to begin with. That is their purpose in the story. And so, a great change is brought about, without any forced change at all. Equality becomes like water: it's fluid. And of course, I am not trying to romanticize/downplay the true struggle of people of color during Victorian times. I'm aware it was hell. The Pitchers involvement in this is not as much a depiction of racial relationships in Victorian times, as they are a reflection of modern times, and what we have to undergo. If you spot difference, then overcome any discomfort you may have, then just learn, read a story where there are many races/nationalities, and can enjoy it without any apprehension, you are a hero, in your own right. That's the point. Because that's the best place to start. It's all the little things in life...

I hope you can understand these reasons for why I do what I do. But those who have read this far into the series are no fools, so I know that you understand. Whether you agree or not is entirely up to you. Remember, you don't have to agree with me, but I'll still love you all, all the same.

But now this explanation can prepare you for anytime I ever present different races into the narrative of my books. It is *never* meant to polarize or make anyone apprehensive about a guilt trip story. It's because it's natural to bring other types into tales, because that is how the world is structured... and because I'm a child from the 80s; different cultures look pretty against each other. From a literary standpoint, we're all like a foil for each other. It creates pretty pictures sometimes. And I can't help it... I'm a sucker for beauty.

Thanks again, and in the words of the show 'The Prisoner': Be Seeing You!

— Ney Mitch

THANK YOU FOR READING

Did you enjoy this book?

We invite you to leave a review at your favorite book site, such as Goodreads, Amazon, Barnes & Noble, etc.

DID YOU KNOW THAT LEAVING A REVIEW...

- Helps other readers find books they may enjoy.
- Gives you a chance to let your voice be heard.
- Gives authors recognition for their hard work.
- Doesn't have to be long. A sentence or two about why you liked the book will do.

About the Author

Ney Mitch has been a long-standing Jane Austen enthusiast, having written forty novels that were inspired by her various works. Since stumbling on Miss Austen's books after graduating from college, she has always dabbled in Austen inspired literature, ranging from writing works for teens to adults. Originally, her desire was to adapt Jane Austen's writing in a way to help young adults connect with her, however over time, she has spread her aims to other genres and styles. Having received her BA Degree at Desales University, she is a writer, both literary and dramatic, as well as being a Historic Reenactor.

facebook.com/courtney.mitchell.589

x.com/CMMitchelPsyche

pinterest.com/shebaanna

Moments of Moments Present

Moments of Moments Future

Moments of Moments Infinite

Pride & Prejudice & New Adventures

Rapture & Rebellion

Fortune & Misfortune

Desire & Destiny

Pride & Peace

Resolve & Revelations

Hope & Hopelessness

Faith & Family

Chances Series

Chances Are

Chances Come

Chances Fade

Chances End

Novels

The Tale of Mr. & Mrs. Bennet: A Pride & Prejudice Christmas Tale

Considerations Near Christmastime